The Reticent

(Cathy's Story)

By

J.E.Martin

Copyright ©2019

All rights reserved. No part of this publication may be reproduced, distributed, or transmitted in any form or by any means, including photocopying, recording, or other electronic or mechanical methods, without the prior written permission of the publisher, except in the case of brief quotations embodied in critical reviews and certain other noncommercial uses permitted by copyright law.

Disclaimer

This is a work of fiction. Names, characters, businesses, places, events, locales, and incidents are either the products of the author's imagination or used in a fictitious manner. Any resemblance to actual persons, living or dead, or actual events is purely coincidental.

Cover design: ACG Design

Other books from the 'When Darkness Calls' series:-

- Sold Out/Soul Doubt (book 1)
- Sold Out Too (book 3)
- The Reticent Witch ('The Years of Forlorn Absolution' mini-series)

For Jacqueline with love always.

To all my friends and family who have continued to support and dare I say encourage me on my journey. Particularly my ex-wife Debbie and son Thomas. Thank you.

A special thank you to my beautiful friend Eve who adorns the front cover of this book, but who is in no way, shape or form an actual Witch. (honest)

Also thank you to Susana Rio and Lauri Allen for your feedback and for taking the time to help out a total stranger who stalked you on Insta. Perhaps the human race is not yet doomed.

Chapter 1
A Star is Born

I was born on the 7th of June 1983 at 7:06 a.m. After a perfectly healthy pregnancy, followed by a short and uneventful labour.

My name— Catherine Antionette Heely. Weighing in at six pounds, eight ounces.

As I grew older, I would often wonder if I should have arrived a day earlier so as to be sixth of the sixth. The Darkness that I felt resided within me was intense. Perhaps the seven signified a little good to balance the evil that I felt lived inside of me. The fact my time of birth was also 7:06 made it seem even odder. Though I guess around the world each year thousands of people will be born on the 7th June at 7:06. *It's funny isn't it how we try to find links where perhaps there are none—* My hateful little sister did say that I was born at 6:66. *The bitch had to go and spoil it.*

I was born to Robert and Sallyanne Heely. My father, a self-employed landscape gardener; my mother, a part-time librarian.

The look on my father's face when it was announced I was a beautiful and healthy girl, would stay with me. My father had wanted a boy. Perhaps had he gotten his wish this might have been a very different story indeed. Probably not for the better. I am sure of it.

Wait a minute, I am a newborn, how could I see, remember and interpret the look on my father's face? Well, you might already be aware that I am far from an *average* child.

Apparently, I am pretty, with a thick head of raven hair and dark hazel eyes, the general consensus is that I look like my mother, *Sally*. It turns out that I share more than just my looks with her.

My sister Linda is three, my arrival does not go down well with her. Linda's need to have all the attention would be her constant Achilles heel throughout her troubled life.

From the very start, Linda would give me a little nip or tug my hair when she thought no one was looking. Deliberately wake me from my sleep and generally, be a spiteful and horrid little girl.

I was eighteen months old when the Darkness first called to me. I was sat in my highchair eating whatever slop was in my bowl, making a mess; as usual my face and bib covered in the contents of the dish.

My horrid sister, seeing my mother had her back turned, leant over from her chair and spat in my food; quickly sitting back, with a smirk on her face.

Not even aware of what was happening, I heard a voice whisper words I couldn't know— yet I did. I locked eyes with my sister, and moments later, Linda was projectile vomiting all over the kitchen. Simultaneously soiling herself as she retched uncontrollably.

'Oh my god,' shouted my mum.

Linda was screaming in distress between her bouts of retching. I cannot believe just how much vomit could be emitted from such a small child.

As my mother tried to console Linda, she instinctively looked at me. I was banging the tray of my highchair with the spoon and giggling hysterically. At that point, my mother knew.

Quickly, my mother gathered us up and off we went to A&E. Eventually, we were seen, and it was soon determined that my poor sister had gastroenteritis. No cure and no apparent cause, just plenty of water and light meals until it passed.

I'm not sure Linda ever connected the dots, perhaps if she had, it would have saved her from what would eventually be in store for her. But that said, she seemed a little less spiteful from that point on.

Chapter 2
Sibling Rivalry

Although Linda seemed to back-off with her physical torment of me, she focussed instead on vying for love and attention and generally trying to be number one in everyone's eyes.

As I mentioned previously, this would backfire on her constantly. Sometimes in the most horrendous of ways, and without any intervention from me.

Linda needed constant praise and validation. It became a competition, 'dad loves me more than he loves you,' she would often taunt. She would sit by his side on the sofa, cuddle in as close as possible and kiss him constantly.

I could see how conflicted it made my dad. Happy on the one hand that his daughter loved him so. Yet also uncomfortable with how it might look to outsiders, he became quite self-conscious of it, even within the home environment.

It was painful to watch; as Linda acted out on her insecurities. Dad would even lose his temper and be quite short with her at times. But she just never let up.

I felt an overwhelming urge to intervene. But how?

In the end, at the age of ten, and after much deliberation and research. I decided to give Linda allergic rhinitis. Making her particularly allergic to grass pollen, something dad was always covered in. She would immediately go into anaphylaxis. The first attack was quite acute; resulting in her being hospitalised; as a result she was issued with an EpiPen.

The eventual conclusion meant she needed to steer clear of dad. Sublime really.

Linda now had to find new and inventive ways to get one over on me. *Bring it on sis.*

I was a good student at school. I didn't have to try too hard to make the grade. My genetics honed over centuries saw to that. I was an A-grade student in Art, Biology, Languages and History.

It would seem that history books are primarily works of fiction. Written to hide the truth. Written to manipulate the masses; in many ways, the same as modern religion.

Linda was less academic than I was. Not stupid by any stretch of the imagination. Just not close to my level of attainment.

The information stored in our DNA is boundless. Unfortunately, our brains cannot access this information readily. Occasionally a child genius like Wolfgang Amadeus Mozart comes along. He is accessing past experiences from his gene pool. Not to be confused with a past life.

Wild animals can instinctively do things they have never been taught. They can recognise danger and predators without any prior knowledge. It's the same principle.

I can access all the information locked away in my DNA. All that had been passed down through my carefully selected bloodline.

Initially though, I would liken it to looking at the contents of your computer hard drive in the form of machine code or binary. The older I got, the more adept I became at accessing and understanding it. With a little help here and there from my ever-present mentor and tormentor; The Darkness.

Linda's latest strategy was to try and either steal my friends or to spread lies about me; continually trying to undermine me. Her actions did probably help in alienating me from the masses. Though I didn't really care. The bullying I could have done without as this did tap into my dark side.

Linda's actions meant we never grew any closer than hating each other's guts. We eventually learned to tolerate one another, but there was no closeness. Though as my flesh and blood, I did still love her. She was damaged, a jealous, spiteful girl. That's how I compartmentalised it to get past it.

Chapter 3
Like Mother, Like Daughter

I was ten when mother dear decided to first take me to one side, for a *little chat*.

It was a lovely summers day, dad was working, and Linda and I were playing in the garden; Not together, I hasten to add. Linda was on the swing at the bottom of the garden.

I was sitting on the second of the five half-moon shaped steps that led from the French doors down to the lawned area of the garden. I say lawned. Dad had astroturfed it to reduce the impact on Linda.

In my hand was my sketchbook, I was drawing a Mistle Thrush that was perched on the stone birdbath. I enjoyed drawing, and I loved nature. I always felt at one with it.

Suddenly startled the Thrush flew directly towards me, over my head and into the kitchen through the open French doors.

Realising its error, it turned and flew back, but not through the French doors. Instead, it flew into the closed kitchen window above the sink.

Landing on the tiled floor, it had broken its neck, one wing was stuck out awkwardly to one side, the other tucked in neatly.

I gathered it up, so soft and warm, its head drooped over to one side, and its beak open slightly.

What happened next was an automatic, almost involuntary action. I cupped the bird gently in my hand and moved it closer to my face. I then blew into its partially open beak.

Suddenly the bird was alive in my hands. Quickly running to the garden, I placed it carefully on the edge of the birdbath, its poor head still floppy.

Almost immediately, all the birds in the surrounding trees seemed to start shrieking; then out of the sky descended several Crows.

The Crows attacked the Thrush. They tore it to shreds to the sound of my screams; eventually leaving a mess of blood, guts and feathers.

By now Linda was screaming, having heard the commotion and seeing the horror.

Mother appeared.

'Oh, my!' She started, 'what on earth has happened here?'

I sobbed out a mostly incoherent response from which she seemed to conveniently glean, that some Crows had attacked another bird and killed it.

Linda had fortunately, not seen the preceding events. Darling Mother, on the other hand, had heard my explanation in full.

After we had calmed down from the traumatic scene we had witnessed, Linda went back out to the garden.

Taking me through to the lounge and seating me on the sofa, my mother looked at me with a look of slight fear and trepidation.

'Cathy —' she started, 'Cathy, you have a unique ability. You know that, don't you?'

I knew exactly what she meant, and she knew I knew. A somewhat surreal moment— I nodded as I often did —

'Yes,' I replied, 'am I evil?' I asked sheepishly.

'Oh, darling, not at all, I have a special gift too— and I'm not a bad person, am I?'

This was true. My mother was quite an accomplished Medium, but her powers or gift ended there. Mine were growing in magnitude almost daily, and I was starting to worry about what I might become.

'Do you have the same *gift* as me mum?' *already knowing the answer.*

'No, Cathy, you have far greater powers than me,' she replied, changing the reference from *gift* to *powers*.

'And what does that mean mum?' I asked quizzically.

'It means you must be careful; you must learn to control them and at the same time to hide them from other people.'

'Why? — If they're not bad. Why do I need to hide them?' I asked, but again knowing the answer.

'Because people won't understand, they will be afraid of you. People fear what they don't understand.'

'So does Linda have it too?' I asked, purely out of a sense of smug spite.

'No, Cathy— but then you knew that already. Look I have books that can help you develop and manage your gifts, help you to understand them more. I will help you.'

'But I don't want these gifts, mum.'

It was true, they already frightened me, I had tested them previously, and my power over the natural world seemed already well developed.

'I'm sorry baby, the best you can do is learn to control them and not allow them to control you.'

'They scare me, mum,' I said softly. 'So why did the Crows kill that Thrush that I brought back to life?' I continued, 'That was awful.'

'That's because it should not have been brought back, it had no soul, it was an abomination against nature and had to be killed.'

'Then why do I have the power if I can't use it to save things?' I asked; genuinely puzzled as to why this power exists if it cannot be used.'

'It is known as necromancy — you are a necromancer.'

'A nec-ro-man-cer.' I sounded out. 'What does that mean?'

'In simple terms Cathy, it means that you are an extraordinary witch, you have the power to raise the dead— you must be very careful as your powers are drawn from the dark realm, and the Darkness will try to make you use your powers for evil.'

I froze momentarily as those words sank in— Witch, Darkness— Evil. It's not every day at age ten, that you get told you are a powerful witch.

'But witches aren't real mum, even I know that.'

'But you know what you did, Cathy. How do you explain it? You are a witch.'

'What is the Darkness?'

'Well many might call it evil or even the devil, but it is much more than that. You have heard the Darkness, that is why you made your sister sick. You were angry with her for something, and the Darkness coerced you to use your powers to hurt her.'

'She spat in my food, mum.'

'Good lord, you weren't even two at the time, and you remember it.'

'I remember everything. Even being inside your womb mum.'

There was an awkward silence as she processed what I was telling her.

'Oh Cathy, you will be able to do so much, if you harness your powers for good. It will have been centuries since a witch, even close to your abilities will have walked the earth,' replied my mother proudly.

'I don't want the responsibility. I have already hurt my sister, and I know when I am angry, I feel like I want to punish people. I am scared that I will really hurt someone one day.'

'We will work together to help you manage your powers. Cathy, you need to learn to count to ten, you get your short temper from your dad, and it is crucial you learn to control that over anything else, or I fear the Darkness will corrupt you beyond repair.'

'What do you mean corrupt me beyond repair?'

'Listen Cathy the voice you hear will come to you at the times of your greatest anger or fear. It will try and encourage you to do evil.'

'But why?'

'Because if you strike out and kill someone. The Darkness will own your soul.'

This was pretty heavy shit to hear age ten. My comprehension of things though good, was still growing, this was somewhat overwhelming for me. Though I suppose it's not easy to dress it up and make it more palatable.

'Will he ever stop?'

'Once you reach the age of twenty-one, you will no longer succumb to his suggestions. You will have total control.'

'Why twenty-one?'

'It's the sum of the holy trinity, three times seven, it really is the key to the door Cathy. You must still be careful about how you use your powers.'

'Will it get worse before then?'

'The worst time for you will be between the age of fourteen and twenty-one, eighteen being the most dangerous age. That is the sum of the unholy trinity, three sixes.'

Well, that was reassuring. I was if not careful, going to become an instrument of Hell. Some overzealous avenging angel. I was going to sleep much better knowing all of this.

'I have many books you can read; we will learn together; you must hide them from your father and sister. Your father is very much opposed to my use of the gift. We will chat about this when we are alone. Do not mention this to anyone.'

I again nodded to signify my understanding of her request. I already got called a witch because of my raven hair and dark eyes. Imagine how much more teasing and bullying I would be subjected to if I told people I was a powerful witch. God help me — but then god help them, if their taunting made me angry.

Being told you effectively have superpowers at age ten, is quite something I can tell you. Coupled with the age-related immaturity, the temptation to show off one's superpowers was immense. Indeed, I almost felt cheated that I had to keep them a secret. But then I guess that's what superheroes do. I wonder what my costume would be, certainly not a black cape, pointy hat and broomstick, that's for sure.

Chapter 4
Hard Times of 93

As I approached eleven years of age, our family fell on hard times. Dad was short of work, and as the primary earner, it meant we had to tighten our belts.

They do say that when the money stops coming through the door, love flies out of the window. The strain was undoubtedly starting to show.

My father knew of my mothers' gift. However, he did his best to discourage her from using it. Though not particularly religious, he felt that it was black magic. He was unaware that I too had the gift.

I had used my gift to help my dad, without him knowing. We had a huge garden which had two large greenhouses. My dad liked to grow his own bedding plants and dabbled with grafting and developing new blooms. His endeavours were covertly aided by me. I was interested and he would tell me what it was he was aiming for. Needless to say, he was extremely successful in this enterprise winning many awards at local and national level.

Anyway, as a result of the ever more precarious financial situation; mum had decided to start performing spiritual readings for people. A little extra tax-free cash would help plug the gap in our current finances.

Because mum was good— very good in fact; word soon spread, and she was making good money. This, in itself, did not sit well with her ethically. She did not believe that *the gift* should be used for personal gain. But family comes first, I guess.

Her now well-known powers of mediumship did increase the bullying and teasing I experienced at school. *I just had to suck it up.*

Mum had told us that she had managed to find the odd cleaning jobs here and there to supplement her hours at the library.

It wasn't long though before dad found out. I think he had suspected. Mums earnings were far higher than that of a cleaner doing an extra 16 hours per week. In fact, she was earning more than my dad had when he had been busy.

A combination of good old male pride, anger at being disobeyed and a skin full of alcohol resulted in a blazing row. This was a first. It scared me. Linda ran off to her bedroom crying. I stood in disbelief as the argument escalated.

Dad had mum cornered. His left hand holding her by the throat.

'I told you I don't want you doing that shit— it's evil— you're evil,' he shouted.

'It's not evil, Bob— I help people,' she managed to croak in response.

'No— It's the devil's work.'

'No, dad. Stop it. It's not evil— I have it too, I'm like mum,' I interjected cautiously.

'What! — You've been teaching our daughter!'

My comment had the opposite effect to that intended. Rather than calming my father, it enraged him more.

'Witch,' he shouted as he struck my mum with the back of his right hand; sending her reeling toward me.

As he raised his hand ready to strike her again, I grabbed his leg. He instinctively grabbed my hair and pulled my head back— his other arm drawn in preparation to hit me. As I looked up at this man— this man I loved and respected with all my heart. I felt it— I heard it— I acted on it.

The next thing I knew, my dad was laid on the floor. Unresponsive but breathing. Mum called an ambulance; but not before looking at me with sorrow. Dad was rushed to the hospital. We were informed he had suffered a catastrophic stroke and that he would be lucky to survive.

He did survive. He was almost completely paralysed, unable to speak, communicating only by blinking his eyes.

I was devastated by what I had done.

My dad was a mere empty shell of the man he once was. He and mum had oft-spoken about what-ifs. What if I were in a vegetative state? Would you turn off the life-support? We have all had those discussions. I knew what my dad wanted.

In the end, I could take no more. Seeing my father fully cognizant, trapped in a lifeless body was too much. After only a month or so, I decided to end his suffering.

'Morning, dad. I have your breakfast,' I said as I entered his bedroom.

He looked at me as he always did, with a mixture of love, hate and regret.

Sitting on the chair at his bedside, I placed the bowl of cereal on the unit by his bed.

'I think it's time to say, goodbye, dad, don't you?' I asked softly.

One blink for yes or two for no. He blinked slowly and deliberately — one blink.

A tear rolled down his cheek.

'I'm sorry dad. Can you forgive me?' I asked softly.

One more slow, deliberate blink.

'I forgive you too, dad, I do love you, and if I could undo what I have done, I would. In fact, I have tried.'

I moved so that I could look him directly in his eyes, we locked gazes as we had when I had struck him down. He forced the slightest of smiles and again blinked once.

The bleed that followed was colossal and killed him instantly.

Chapter 5
Let's Chat

The next serious chat I had with my mum was— you guessed it— after I'd struck down my father. Linda had gone to stay at friends. Dad was in bed. It was the week after my father's release from the hospital.

'Cathy, come and sit with me,' said my mum from the living room; as I walked past, heading to the kitchen for a drink.

I poured myself a glass of milk and dutifully proceeded to the living room.

'What's up?' I asked nonchalantly.

'Why did you do that to your father?'

'Because.'

'Don't play silly games. Why such a severe punishment? He didn't deserve what you did.'

'I don't want to say.'

She looked at me with a knowing in her eyes. *Easy to forget she has gifts too.*

'It wasn't me, mum, it was the Darkness.'

'That's no excuse, Cathy. You should fight it.'

'But I can't when I'm scared or angry, it just takes over. I didn't want to hurt dad. But he was going to hit me and hit me hard. I read his thoughts; he was thinking; *I'll beat the devil out of this one.*

'You did let your anger take over.'

'You don't know what it's like to have this curse. You are nothing compared to me. You don't know the Darkness!'

As my short venomous tirade ended, I was unsure if mum was going to cry or strike me in anger.

'I'm sorry, Cathy. I do understand your plight. You must be stronger and smarter than this.'

'I wish I could undo what I have done,' I said, as I started to cry.

'I know baby it's okay, don't cry,' she said, as she hugged me tightly.

'I can't help acting out when I'm scared or angry.'

'I think we need to get you some counselling or something to help you manage your emotions. Otherwise, you will be consumed by the Darkness.'

That as they say was that. At age ten, I was having specialist sessions of CBT and anger management counselling. I will say that it did help. *Don't knock it until you've tried it*. I guess I apply that maxim to most aspects of my life.

The sessions were productive, giving me coping strategies to help defuse situations before they escalated to the point I would strike out. I was always empathetic. But I could go from being the most caring person you could ever meet, to being your worst nightmare incarnate, in a matter of seconds.

My mum had seen a business card on the community notice board at work. It was for a hypnotist, stop smoking, help with phobias, and so on. Having spoken to the hypnotist a Mr Dawson, the poor unsuspecting man had agreed to try and help.

As I was a minor, he insisted quite rightly that my mother be present. He would also video the session; for further legal protection, I assume.

We arrived at his home, where he had an area that had been converted to a pleasant little consultation and treatment room. Pictures and statues of Brahma and the like adorned the softly lit space. The only thing that seemed to be missing was a CD of whale calls playing in the background.

Mr Dawson explained the process and tried to establish what our aims were. Obviously, we didn't tell him I was a witch— a witch who had a resident evil within her— No! — We said I had anger issues and that maybe these were deep-seated from a previous traumatic experience, that I was subconsciously blocking out.

Poor Mr Dawson decided he would try a little hypnotic regression. Perhaps the unlicensed practice of hypnosis needs to be more tightly regulated!

Mr Dawson was a nice man and did not abuse his ability. But he had no clue as to what was about to happen. Nor did we, for that matter.

We did the standard count backwards, having first secured my mind in its safe place. At the point I should have been in a light trancelike sleep— my eyes opened wide.

Mr Dawson was now in direct contact with the Darkness. It would seem my minds safe place was the bowels of hell.

What follows is my mum's recollection. We never received the video footage from poor Mr Dawson. Nor strangely did it ever appear on YouTube.

My eyes did not suddenly glow red— No! — My dark hazel eyes did dilate fully. Now I am not at this point technically possessed— Though I do have what seems to be a spiritual hotline to the Darkness.

I have little or no control over this. It tends to leave me be. Unless that is, I get angry or scared. I was most certainly not angry. I was, however, a little apprehensive about the hypnosis. Maybe even a little scared.

My mum, however, did liken my demeanour to that of someone who was possessed.

I looked straight back at Mr Dawson. He immediately felt a little unnerved as this was not typical of someone in a hypnotic state.

'Now Cathy, I would like you to go backwards in time to your earliest memory,' suggested Mr Dawson.

'How far back do you want me to go? — To the dawn of time or the birth of man; maybe even his expulsion from the garden of Eden?' the Darkness replied. It's voice deep and guttural.

Mr Dawson had certainly not expected that, as I grinned at him menacingly. Mr Dawson must have thought he was reliving a scene from the Exorcist. Bless him though, he tried to style it out.

'Is that what you think you are Cathy? — The devil?'

'I am the sum of all your fears,' I hissed.

'No, you are just a frightened and confused little girl Cathy.'

'You have no business here, there is nothing to see, nothing that can be fixed.'

'Okay Cathy I am going to now count to five, and when I reach five, you will be back with us.'

Mr Dawson had seen and heard enough.

'You have no power here. I will decide when this is over, not you.'

Regardless Mr Dawson counted to five. I laughed heartily with an almost theatrical evil laugh.

I then looked at Mr Dawson. He was scared. He was right to be. I was laid bare. I had no control. I was completely unaware of the situation we were in. The Darkness could kill him and chalk it up to me.

Mr Dawson had several large candles lit, all part of the mood-setting. He also had a crystal Brahma, not a cheap keepsake from a holiday to India. No! This was expensive. The real deal.

Suddenly the candles were all blown out. A real horror movie cliché I know. But hey that's what happened. Next, the crystal Brahma simply exploded as I sat there and grinned like the Joker from the batman movies.

At that moment, I was back in the room. Looking at two terrified people. I was at a loss, shattered bits of Brahma everywhere. Mr Dawson looked as though he might still die of fright.

'What's wrong?' I asked innocently. 'What's happened?'

'I think you should leave now,' said Mr Dawson. This was clearly not a request.

'I'm so sorry,' replied my mum.

'It's not a hypnotist you need Mrs Heely, it's an exorcist,' said Mr Dawson, 'please don't come back again,' he continued as he shut and locked his door behind us.

'What's an exorcist mum?'

'Oh, never mind that baby, Mr Dawson is clearly a fraud.'

I was in my late teens before mum gave me the low-down on my session with Mr Dawson

Chapter 6
Confessions

A few days after my failed hypnosis, mother dear again requested I sit with her for a chat.

Dad was in bed, his days numbered. *Though he didn't know that.*

Linda was out with one of her bitchy mates. *Doubtless sat bitching and plotting against me and others that they were jealous of.*

'Cathy—I have not been candid with you about my own powers.'

'What do you mean, mum— are you the same as me, after all?'

'No! — Not even close. But I too hear the Darkness.'

'Does he try and make you do bad things?'

'No— he talks about you.'

'What does he say.'

'He has plans for you, which you know already. He desires your soul and your allegiance to him.'

'So why not tell me that himself?'

'He wants me to help you develop your powers. Your father stifled me during my formative years. I could have been so much more. Nowhere near what you can be though.'

'How do you mean dad stifled you.'

'We met at school, your dad was my first and only boyfriend, we were in love.'

'So how did that stifle you?'

'I had told your dad about my gift. He was opposed to me using it. He believed it was evil, and he made me promise to suppress it. I did it because I loved him.'

'So why don't you tell the Darkness you're not willing to do what he asks?'

'Because he is using threats.'

'What threats?'

'I can't say. Trust me though he means it.'

'Maybe I should just kill myself and have done with it.'

'You can't.'

'Why not?'

'Cathy, you will either die of natural causes or at the hands of the Darkness.' Nothing, man nor beast will ever be allowed to harm you.'

'What? — Do you mean I am immortal?'

'No! just that the Darkness will do whatever is needed to protect you.'

'So, he is like a bodyguard?'

'Yes, I guess you could say that.'

'Cool!'

'Not really is it Cathy?'

'Sorry.'

'Look, he has two objectives. He will try and coerce you to kill an innocent, this will continue until you are twenty-one and will require you to be strong and vigilant. Secondly, he will protect you until you willingly give yourself to him or until the day that you die.'

'Is that why he struck dad down?'

'No! I know you were scared, but your father was no risk to your life. Now that your father is aware you have the gift. The Darkness did not want him to do to you what he had done to me.'

'So, it is my fault for telling dad I had the gift too?'

'No— you did what you thought was right to protect me.'

'But it wasn't right.'

'Look if you are in danger, if you fear for your life, he will intervene and through you, he will eliminate the threat by whatever means your powers will allow.'

'Then that surely makes me dangerous to be around.'

'No, it doesn't. Only for people who wish you harm. What you must be careful of is your anger. That is within your control. It allows the Darkness in; it allows him to influence your actions. This is where your vigilance is imperative, or you will kill an innocent.

'So, I can't pick up that knife and slit my wrists with it?'

'Why don't you try?'

My mother's response frightened me. Was she really saying that I couldn't or just that I wouldn't?'

'I jumped up from the table and pulled out the large cook's knife from the knife block. I looked at mum defiantly, and with absolute intent, I tried to cut my wrist. It was as though someone had hold of my arm. I was unable to make contact with my wrist. As hard as I tried, I was prevented from doing so.

'I told you,' she said, as I placed the knife back in the block.

So, it would seem that I have the Prince of Darkness as my own personal bodyguard. Despite mum's earlier admonishment of my comment. *How awesome is that?*

Chapter 7
The Witches Apprentice

I was not sent to Hogwarts. No such luck. No! I attended a mediocre primary, followed by an equally mediocre secondary.

My schooling for all thing's witchcraft was done at home. My mum, as I said, was a gifted medium, but that was pretty much all she had in her bag of tricks. Though her knowledge on the subject was comprehensive.

My mother worked part-time at the local library. She had a wealth of books on the subject of — well— of witchcraft actually.

All things conjuration and necromancy. I got a distinct feeling that mother dear, wished that she had the gifts that I had. Maybe even that she could learn them from me.

I'm not quite sure where some of the books had been sourced. Certainly not from the easy reading section of the local library; of that, I was in absolutely no doubt.

We would study together when alone. Mum would make excuses saying I was struggling with my schoolwork, encouraging dad and Linda to vacate the house whenever possible.

I really enjoyed our study time. Not just because I was learning about my powers; but because I really enjoyed history. It does seem that the powers that be, have tried hard to eradicate from history or at least the school curriculum, any mention of the so-called occult.

It seems that I may well be related to John Dee or moreover his wife and Edward Kelly. John Dee was a mathematical and scientific genius; he would be considered a great mind if he were alive today. Yet his accomplishments are hidden or ignored because he dabbled in the occult. Science dismisses him as do the mainstream religions. He is effectively in a no-mans-land. Dee was an advisor to Queen Elizabeth I who as well as being referred to as the virgin queen was also known as the witch or fairy queen.

Another monarch James I also does not get the attention that he deserves, we all know about Henry VIII all he did was have loads of wives. James I commissioned the English translation of the bible the KJV this was pivotal, he also introduced the Act against Witchcraft and Conjuration, authored a book called daemonologie and was unfortunately instrumental in the witch hunts and witch trials. He was also the target of the Guy Fawkes plot. So much went on during this period as Nostradamus was also active during the sixteenth century.

Dee was instrumental in developing navigational aids that made it possible to discover the New World, the New World had only just been discovered yet Nostradamus predicted the fall of the twin towers.

It seems that since then scientists and historians alike have worked to hide these events from mainstream history or simply discredit them.

Consider that Dee and King James I. spoke fluently not only English but Latin, Greek and several other languages. These were not uneducated fools who believed in ghosts and the like. These were highly intelligent men who even today would be revered for their intellect.

It was due to my interest in Dee and Kelly that I was drawn to scrying. Scrying requires the use of a black mirror, in some respects, it is similar to using a crystal ball. It allows communication with the otherwise unseen spirit world.

There are conflicting opinions as to whether you look inward or whether it opens a direct window to the world of Angels and Demons.

I find that you do need to prepare your mind, but then once your mind is open, then a window does open up. Dee documented many cases where full manifestations occurred and interacted directly with himself and Kelly.

I was always fascinated by Dee's obsession with an Angel by the name of Madimi, and I tried many times without success to communicate with her. Not until much later in my life did I finally manage to make contact.

Dee and Kelly had documented over seventy different Angels or Demons over a period of seven years. My early attempts were at times unsettling, and a number of my communications were with what appeared to be demons, some in a human-like form others not.

Consequently, I put away the black mirror until I was much older, more experienced and confident in my abilities.

I continued to research Madimi. Some speculate she was a demon in disguise. She was one of the seven children of Galvah the angel of light. However, Lucifer translates to the morning star, and he was the original angel of light.

It was Madimi who insisted Dee and Kelly crossmatch as it was called. Effectively wife swap. This marked the end of the angelic conversations as Dee struggled with doing as

Madimi had instructed— he and Kelly would part company shortly afterwards.

Key to my development was learning to read the data stored in my DNA; this was everything ever experienced by everyone in my direct bloodline all the way back to the dawn of man.

We are all walking history books. If only everyone could access this. The possibilities would be endless.

The key was learning to search this internal database as it would be impossible to ever recall or sift through it all. So, a little like 'type here to search' at the bottom corner of your computer screen.

The older I got the more proficient I became. I was always picked for the pub quiz team. Although some of my answers were at odds with the quizmaster as I was correct, he was taking his answers from the inaccurate history books of modern-day.

My most significant powers, in addition to the range of 'Clairs' that I had; was my ability to affect any living thing. I could easily manipulate any living organism and its biological function.

As a witch I have what is known as *the evil eye;* this you are born with, it cannot be taught, Sorcery is a different thing altogether; sorcery can be learned.

There is much written about the *evil eye*; witches who could cause harm to animals, men and even crops with just a look.

Some of my magic required me to touch the target, the most powerful magic required me to consume blood or other bodily fluids.

It was the *evil eye* that I most needed to control. Its potential was vast. It could be administered as quickly as pulling the trigger of a gun. The consequences devastating or even fatal.

Quite literally in the blink of an eye, I could end life. It was this power that the Darkness would attempt to coerce me to use in moments of fear or anger. I had to be prepared. I had to be vigilant, and I had to be strong.

Chapter 8
School Bully

It was not long after the incident with my father that I found myself attracting unwanted attention from one of the many school bullies.

Young Thomas Crossland and his gang of two, all wannabe gangsters were making their way over to where I was sat. I got up from the bench and began to walk away.

The girls of my age avoided me mostly. They were not particularly mean. I guess on reflection I did look a little like Wednesday Adams; and having what these days is lovingly referred to as; *resting bitch face.*

Rumours had got out that my mum was a medium. So now I was Carrie as well as the usual Morticia, Wednesday Adams or Lily Munster. You get the picture I'm sure.

Kids are so inventive. Obviously, their parents had made comments too; based on the fact that the majority of their comparisons were coming from nineteen-sixties TV characters. Carrie though! —Little did they know.

Thomas was the absolute archetypal school bully. A little overweight, or maybe just big-boned. Not blessed with the best looks or highest IQ in the school. Product of a broken home and with insecurities oozing from his every sweaty pore. If he'd been ginger; that I'm sure would have finished him off.

'Hey, Carrie,' shouted Thomas, 'Have you started your periods yet?'

Thomas and his two sycophantic dullard mates all laughed at his incredible wit.

I took a deep breath, counted to ten as instructed by my mum, and my various counsellors; ignored him and walked on.

'Hey. I'm talking to you Blair Witch,' he again shouted. Seemingly, his drollness had no end.

I stopped and turned to face him. Thomas was in the same year as me, a little older, a couple of inches taller and a good few pounds heavier.

'What's up Cartmen?' I replied with a smirk. His two mates resisted the urge to grin at my comment. Instead, they looked to Thomas to see what he might do or say to this insulant little witch.

Thomas chose to completely ignore my remark.

'I said, have you started your period yet Carrie?'

As it turned out, young Thomas was remarkably timely with his comment; as I had the previous week at the tender age of ten; indeed, started my periods. Unlike Carrie from the movies, it had been no big deal to me, my mother or anyone else for that matter. I was not, however, about to discuss my menstrual cycle with this moron.

'Grow up, Thomas, have you had a wet dream yet?' I replied.

'Shut it, Carrie!'

'Look, fat boy, I'm really not in the mood so jog on before I go all Carrie on you.'

My fat boy comments clearly touched a nerve. Thomas stepped forward. Now toe to toe with me.

'What's up Carrie— have you got PMT? — did it run down your legs did it? —

As I looked into his eyes, the Darkness spoke.

'affa tia.' It said. Enochian. I understood it. *Empty him.*

Before I could even think about it, there was suddenly a sound of trickling water.

'What like that?' I replied as I looked down at his wet trousers and the urine pooling by his feet.

His mates could not contain themselves.

Ha, Ha, look! Tommy's pissed his pants,' shouted James one of his Troglodyteian followers.

Poor Thomas. His face a picture of humiliation. He turned and ran away, crying like the baby that he was.

I looked at his two mates, who were momentarily frozen in a trancelike state, having seen their big hard, gangster hero wet himself and then run away like a little girl.

'BOO!' I shouted, at the same time pretending to lunge toward them.

They turned tail and followed in the general direction that Thomas had headed.

I was pleased with myself. This superpower of mine was pretty cool. I guess it is easy to see why Luke's father succumbed to the Darkside to become Darth Vader. The temptation to abuse such power is enormous. More so when a voice in your head is saying, *'empty him.'* In Enochian, a language, I had not been taught, yet understood fully.

I had hoped Thomas would not want to face me after our last encounter. Hopefully, he would be too embarrassed. His two mates had moved on. Presumably not that impressed with a boy who faced with a girl, wets himself and then runs away crying.

I should have been so lucky — he should not have been so stupid! The following week Thomas-no-mates caught me by myself at the back of the art block. I was doing nothing more than sketching an old dead elderflower tree in the school grounds.

He grabbed me firmly by the neck, with a real purpose in his eyes. He then pushed me against the wall.

'Think you're clever little witch, don't you?' he seethed. 'Well I'll show you clever,' he said, his grip tightening slightly.

I wasn't sure if he wanted to kill me or kiss me — I'm not sure that he was either.

However, as we were now in direct contact, I could read him clearly. My powers of mediumship include all the *clairs* you can mention. I could see the obvious that he actually fancied me. Yuk! But I could see beyond the present. I could see that he would continue in his bullying ways and become a wife-beating drunk, much like his father.

Seeing this turned my momentary fear into absolute wrath. The voice in my head was calling out to me to act swiftly and decisively. To *stop* this monster in the making.

As Thomas stared intently into my eyes, his anger evident, he saw into my soul, for the briefest moment, I let him see the Darkness within. His look of anger instantly changing to terror. This was not the Darkness protecting me, this was the Darkness coercing me. By *stop;* It meant me to kill. I wanted him to know that what was coming was absolutely coming from me.

'Bitch!' Was all he managed before dropping to the ground with a seizure. He was rushed to hospital where they found that poor Thomas had contracted meningitis; unfortunately, it was severe, and when he was finally released from the hospital, he was blind and continually dribbling.

I resisted the Darkness and its attempt to coerce me to kill. I could have easily ended his life. I resisted, but I had still lashed out. That was me. I didn't kill. I spared him. Even after giving him a chance previously. But my hormonal changes and the Darkness combined; I was not in total control. I was being seduced. I was starting to get a little power drunk. Not quite sure whether I liked it or not; I was developing a callous and vengeful streak.

After Thomas was released from the hospital, I took the boy some chocolates, *help him to get even fatter*. Telling his parents, I was a school friend named Susie. I think they were shocked. Maybe I had been his only visitor. They were keen to welcome me in. I gave the fake name, as I figured if they had announced me as Cathy, poor Thomas would have had another seizure.

He was sat in a chair, his eyes milky and sightless, drool on his face that his mother wiped away before leaving us.

'I'll let you two chat in private,' she said as she left. 'Can I get you a drink?'

I shook my head. She left.

I walked over to Thomas and leant in to whisper to him.

'Hey Thomas, it's Cathy —'

He went rigid and was about to shout out.

'Shush Thomas or who knows what I might do to you?'

His face filled with panic as tears started to form in those milky, useless eyes.

'What do you want?' He asked softly, as he trembled in fear.

'I had initially come to gloat Thomas. To revel in my handy work. But seeing you like this makes me genuinely sad, for both of us. If I could undo what I have done to you. I would.'

'I hate you!'

'I understand that, Thomas. I hate me too. But you do need to take some responsibility. You intended to hurt me. I had to do something.'

'You made me go blind. Do you think that is fair?'

'Fair— No—but it all just happened so fast.'

'How did you even do this to me? — I saw something in your eyes; it was evil.'

'And the fact that was the last thing you saw also troubles me Thomas— I am truly sorry.'

'Sorry, doesn't make me see again, does it?'

'I know that, Thomas. But can you forgive me? I acted in self-defence.'

I suppose that I was asking a lot of an eleven-year-old boy who was now blind for the rest of his life because of what I had done.

'No— I hate you, Cathy.'

'Did you tell anyone that you thought I did this to you?'

'How can I? I was trying to strangle you. And they would just laugh at me anyway. You really are a witch, aren't you?'

'I don't know what I am Thomas. I am truly sorry, I know that. I hope you believe me? I do understand that you can never forgive me; that is my burden to bear.'

'I hope it keeps you awake at night.'

'You have every right to wish that on me Thomas—I'd best be getting on,' I said.

I moved over to where he was sat. I leant in again and kissed him softly on the lips.

'I am so sorry, Thomas.'

'Thanks for calling Susie, I am sure Thomas enjoyed your company,' said his mother after I'd found her busy in the kitchen. *No doubt cooking up some high fat feast for dear Thomas.* 'Do call again.'

'I will, Mrs Crossland,' I replied; knowing that I never would.

My tutelage continued at home. The more I read, the more I was consumed by my almost limitless powers over the natural world. Some of the books laid down rules that could not be broken. I was never sure whether these were written by someone with a limited understanding or were designed to be a code of practice, with voluntary adherence to them.

Of these so-called rules, I had already established that I could bend some and break others.

It would seem that I do not need a wand. *Who knew*?

As I previously mentioned, If I am close to someone and can look them in their eyes, I have a vast array of things that I can do. If I can physically touch them, then I can do a whole lot more.

The darkest powers drawn from Enochian magic required me to ingest blood or other bodily fluids of the chosen victim.

If I want to affect someone or something outside of my immediate view, then I need to use a spell, typically some ingredients are required for most, but not all.

It does seem to me that the only limiting factor is my imagination.

Boy — that makes me dangerous. A real WMD! A Witch of Mass Destruction!

Chapter 9
The Pubescent Witch

Between the age of ten and probably to the point that I lost my virginity, I did use my powers. I suppose I was testing them surreptitiously. Trying to get a real feel for their potential and mine. Also trying to master self-control in the use of them. My dislike of bullies and my seemingly uncontrollable urge to punish them was strong though. I would often fail the test in this respect. On one occasion with fatal consequences.

I started Secondary school. Lots of new faces. A fresh start. Well, almost. Most of the pupils from my primary school were here too, but at least not in my class.

There was a girl in my class called Alison, a sweet girl. A *typical girl next door* type. Unfortunately, she had quite a significant squint, and she did, as a result, get teased. One particular day I bumped into her in the girl's cloakroom at lunchtime. She was sat crying.

'Hey Ali, what's wrong?'

'I'm sick of being called bozz-eye. That's what!'

'Don't let them get to you,' I replied. Feeling somewhat hypocritical; as I knew in her position what I would have likely done.

'It's Grace Haigh, she won't leave me alone.'

Grace was the female version of Thomas Crossland the boy I had problems with at the age of ten. Grace was a mean and spiteful girl.

'Listen, do you believe in god?'

'I don't know.'

'Do you pray?'

'No. Why?'

'Let me tell you a secret. You must never tell. Do you promise?'

Poor little Alison. She looked at me as if I were some mad woman.

'Okay, I promise,' she said cautiously.

'Right then— when you go to bed tonight, I want you to say a little prayer to an Angel called Madimi— '

'Who is she?'

I had seen much mention of this angel in the books I had been studying, so it seemed quite an obvious choice for me.

'She is a special angel, not many people know about her; I want you to say; *Madimi, daughter of the angel of light. I ask that you make my eyes good and true so that I might better see the light. amen.*'

'Will she fix my eye?'

'Yes, when you wake up in the morning, your eye will be straight. I promise. But it must be our secret, or your eye will go back to how it is now. Do you understand?'

Poor Alison nodded. *Had I just threatened her?* I needed to keep this on the downlow.

Okay, so that should have been an end to it. I could not however, resist what I did next. No encouragement from the Darkness. This was me and me alone.

'Hey, Grace. I need a word with you.'

'What's up Esmerelda?'

'Wow— did you think that one up all by yourself?'

Boy oh boy the irony of it. Esmerelda was a beautiful woman. In fact, I look a lot like the Disney version. The fact she was associated with the hunchback of Notre dame does not make it an insult.

'Yes, I did, actually,' she replied, boastfully.

'Yeah— cos I've never heard that one before.'

'So, what's up, freak?'

'I'll tell you what's up, Grace. You need to stop picking on Alison.'

'Why what you gonna do about it?'

I looked her in the eyes—

'Nothing,' I said sheepishly as I turned and walked away.

'Yeah, that's right walk away before I make you sorry you said anything, bitch.'

The following day Alison came skipping into the form room for registration. Her squint was gone. She looked at me beaming from ear to ear. I put my right index finger to my mouth to signify that she shushes. She nodded with an acknowledging smile.

Grace was absent that morning and did not return until the following week. When she did, she had a patch over one eye. Seemingly she had developed a lazy eye. Not permanent but it took a year for it to right itself.

'Ha, Ha, shiver mi timbers,' I said to her, 'where's your parrot?'

I know, I know— I couldn't leave it could I? but it's like the icing on the cake, and no real harm was done, just a lesson in humility for a nasty little girl.

So, a test of my healing ability and controlled, measured and non-permanent punishment. Pass!

At thirteen, I was enjoying school as best you can while fighting the hormonally induced mood swings. My favourite lesson by far was art. Fortunately, too, my favourite teacher, Miss Sykes, was my art tutor.

If you think back to school, you seldom had any direct physical contact with teachers most times, not even an accidental touch. Miss Sykes was collecting our latest pieces as she arrived at my desk. She made contact with my hand as she took my sketch from me. It lingered long enough for me to sense something amiss.

After the class was dismissed, I stayed back. Closing the classroom door, I approached her desk.

'Hey Cathy, you're missing morning break. Is everything alright?' she asked, as she could see I looked a little upset.

'Miss, I need to tell you something, but you will think it's a bit strange.'

'Cathy, what's wrong is someone picking on you?'

'No Miss,' I started, 'it's not about me, it's about you.'

'What do you mean it's about me?'

'Look, Miss, have you heard what people say about my mum? And the names they call me?' I asked, in an attempt to pave the way.

Pausing a moment, she nodded, clearly feeling a little awkward and embarrassed that she knew.

'They call you witches because your mum is a medium,' she replied. 'Is someone teasing you?'

'No more than usual— Do you believe in the spiritual world, Miss?'

'I would like to. Why?'

'Well, I have some powers too. I keep them secret. My mum says that people are afraid of what they don't understand.'

'Yes, I suppose that is true, Cathy. So, what is it you need to tell me?' She replied, her voice sounding a little shaky as she perhaps expected the worst, given the look on my own face.

'I'm sorry, Miss— but you have a problem with one of your ovaries. I think it may be cancer.'

'What?'

'It is early stages, so if you go for tests, they will be able to cure you.'

'Cathy? — What is wrong with you? Why would you say that?'

'Because it is true, Miss. Please go and see a doctor.'

We had a good student, teacher relationship. I was never disruptive, always did my projects and homework on time and helped tidy up after class. For a moment, all of that seemed forgotten as she tried to work out what sort of evil prank I was pulling.

'I need to report this to the headmaster Cathy. You need help.'

'No, Miss, you need help.' I snapped back at her.

'Don't you dare speak to me like that!'

'Okay let me prove it to you. But you have to swear never to tell.'

We had been using whatever medium we chose, be it paint, pencil, charcoal or pastels. The subject was a vase of fresh mixed flowers. This was a favourite demonstration of mine, I used to do it just because I could.

By now, she was ready to march me to the headmaster's office. But her curiosity thankfully got the better of her.

I pulled the vase of flowers closer.

'Promise me you won't tell anyone.'

'Okay, I promise,' she said, with a look of interest on her face.

With that, I wilted the entire vase of flowers; within thirty seconds they looked as though they had been in the vase for a month.

'Oh, my God,' She said.

This did seem to be the standard response.

'You see— I told you. I really like you, Miss, in a way I love you— I don't want you to die. Please see a doctor.'

The gravity of what she had witnessed and what I had told her started to sink in.

'How can you do that, Cathy?'

'I'm a witch, just like they say I am.'

The rational intellect she possessed simply could not explain what she had seen. She knew it was real. No parlour tricks. This was the real thing.

'Oh, Cathy, I am so sorry that I doubted you.'

'Everyone does Miss.'

'I will see a doctor I promise. And thank you,' she said as she gave me a hug. Tears forming in her eyes, as a result of both my diagnosis and what she had just witnessed.

Miss Sykes did have ovarian cancer. *Not that it was ever in any doubt.* She had six months off for surgery and chemotherapy. Returning to school life with her hair gone.

'Miss,' I said, as I once again decided to hang back after class.

'Cathy, I haven't had a chance to thank you properly— thank you, you saved my life. I will never be able to repay you.'

'Just make sure I get good grades,' I joked.

'You don't need my help in that respect, Cathy.'

'Miss I can make your hair grow back more quickly than it would normally. Be back to normal length in a month.'

'My god— you can do that?' she said, with a look of astonishment.

'Yup,' I replied with a grin.

'Go for it.'

'Do you have a colour preference?' I asked. 'Chemo is known to change hair colour and texture, so say now.'

'Well, I'd quite like a lovely head of raven hair like yours if I'm honest.'

'There is only room for one witch in this class, Miss. Sorry!' I smiled.

'How about a light auburn and maybe a little thicker than it used to be.'

I placed both hands on her head. I looked deep into her eyes.

'There you go,' I said.

'What that's it?'

'Yes — Oh and—

'Oh, and What?' she interrupted with a concerned look on her face.

'Mr Spencer really fancies you, but he is a little shy. He is a good man, I sense it. You would be good together.'

'I thought so— he is cute.'

'He's hot Miss, what you on about,' I replied.

Most of the girls in my year had a crush on Mr Spencer.

'The thing is they say I may be unable to have children as they removed one of my ovaries. That might be an issue.'

I placed my hand instinctively over her remaining ovary. She looked at me.

'That won't be a problem, Miss,' I said with a grin.

Miss Sykes looked at me in awe. Had I really just ensured her future fertility? What more was I capable of? I could read her thoughts. I was just happy to help such a lovely woman, through such difficult times.

We continued on with a regular student-teacher relationship. Our secret safe. Miss Sykes never cut me any slack though— *Good for her.*

Another tick in the box. It felt good to be using my powers to help people. It gave me a fresh perspective on what I had considered a curse. The Darkness was mostly silent now. Maybe he was biding his time. Who knew?

Fourteen and still a virgin. *Only just mind!* There was a lot of pressure. With girls of nine pregnant and in the news. It seemed that I was doing well— I was becoming more and more curious, though.

'Yo, Sabrina,' shouted the voice from behind me.

I was at the bus stop, it was late. 11:00 p.m. I was on my way home from visiting a friend. It was Michael Purvis. Perv for short, entirely appropriate, he was a bit of a letch. He was also known as lurch given his stature, so strangely ironic he was calling me names.

Perv was older, pushing eighteen. He did hang around with younger adolescents. He smoked a bit of cannabis and popped a few pills. A lot of the girls thought he was cool. He played on that. He had taken the virginity of a couple of the girls in my year. *Popped their cherries.* As he liked to call it.

He actually lacked confidence with people his own age. Maybe he felt a sense of power over younger girls. Perhaps he was a sexual predator. I didn't have much time for him, though I would see him at parties. I never had an issue with him personally. I'd be quite happy to converse with him, even have a bit of a laugh. But I never fancied him.

'Sabrina was blonde Perv. So that's a shite comparison.'

'But she is a teenage witch.'

'Yes, thanks for that! I am aware who Sabrina is, I replied, 'what are you loitering about for anyway, Perv?'

'Just been down the pool hall.'

'Nice— you been hustling, have you? I hear you're pretty good,' I Said.

I wanted to keep him on-side so a bit of ego massage after my previous sarcasm couldn't hurt.

'Yeah, I'm not bad,' he said a little bashfully, while at the same time looking pleased with himself. 'What you doing out so late?'

'What do you think I'm doing, perv, I'm stood at a frigging bus stop?' *Oops, there I go again.*

Perv wasn't the sharpest knife in the drawer— what he lacked in brains though, he made up for in size and strength. He liked a fight and had been in trouble with the police a couple of times.

'Have you been to your boyfriends?' he quizzed.

'I don't have one. I've been to Hayley's,' I replied, 'Not that it's any of your business.'

I began to have an uneasy feeling. Perv's body language seemed off. The bus stop was quiet, as were the streets, the streetlights intermittent, though the moon was quite bright.

'Look, Michael. Please don't do what it is you're thinking of doing mate.'

'And what might that be?'

'I'm not sure, but you are making me feel a little nervous.'

'Maybe it's because I turn you on. Maybe you fancy me, but you're scared because you're still a virgin.'

'Perv, be assured I like you as a mate, but I do not fancy you. In fact, I prefer girls,' I said, trying to throw a curveball into the mix.

'Maybe I can help you sort out the confusion you feel,' he replied with a dirty grin. 'I'm good at popping cherries!'

At that moment, I knew exactly where this was heading. *Where the fuck was my bus!*

The bus stop was at the edge of the park. If I were him, I'd drag me over the wall into the unlit park. I was wearing a skirt, just above knee length. So, it would give him easier access to the *prize* than jeans would have. *He was thinking exactly that.*

Before I had time to think he suddenly produced a flick-knife. As it clicked and locked, I looked at it in fear. As he put his spare hand to my throat, I could see his thoughts and intent clearly. He fully intended to force himself on me.

By now, I was on my back in the Darkness and solitude of the park, hidden from sight by a four-foot stone wall.

My skirt had been hitched up, and he had cut off my pants with his knife. He was staring between my legs; it was as if he'd never seen one before.

Next came the sound of his zip, as he fumbled to find his dick. *Clearly, not everything was in proportion.*

'Michael, please don't do this,' I begged, 'It's not too late to stop. I won't say a word if you stop now.'

I needed to defuse this quickly I was scared and angry. If Michael had known what this might unleash. he would have thought twice.

'You won't be saying a word anyway!' he said, looking at the blade of his knife.

I was unsure of exactly what he meant by that. On the face of it though, it sounded as though he was going to kill me— *surely not*!

'The thing is Michael— I do fancy you.'

'What? — you're just saying that to save your neck.'

'No— I do, I was just too shy to say so, you've got a reputation, I thought you'd laugh at me. I'm still a virgin, so I don't know what to do.'

He stopped to process the lies I was spinning, I needed him to believe me. I needed him to calm the fuck down for his own sake, not mine.

'Really? You fancy me?' he said. A grin of satisfaction appearing on his face.

'Of course, who wouldn't. All the girls talk about you.'

I should have won an Oscar for my performance.

'Michael— I don't want to do it like this, If I'm going to let you have my virginity, I want it to be right.'

Michael was stood there. His penis ready for action. They say that a standing cock has no conscience. That was unfortunately about to be proved right.

'No— we're doing it right now,' he insisted. A lurid look upon his face.

'Michael, then at least kiss me first.' This was no longer me talking. *I was now in full bodyguard mode.* I was only now along for the ride.

Michael laid on me, his penis was hard and ready to go as I felt it between my legs. He kissed me, I kissed him back. Hard and passionate. I bit his lip, enough to make it bleed. I needed blood. The Darkness was controlling me. He was ready to unleash hells fury on this stupid unsuspecting idiot. What came next was ultimately out of my control.

Michael pulled away for a moment, wiping his lip.

'You like it rough, do you?' he said. Looking even more enthused.

'Not really,' I replied. My voice sounding a touch demonic.

As they always do. Michael looked at me. He saw my protector, the Darkness smiling back. My pupils fully dilated; my eyes even darker than usual. A window to my soul? No! A window into hells fury. I cannot be sure exactly what it is that people see at that moment. I can only surmise from the look of absolute dread that it is as far away from pleasant as it is possible to get. Michael was no different. He jumped to his feet, recoiling in sheer terror at what he saw.

The angel magic used by the Darkness was the most powerful I have ever used. The look on Michael's face as he realised I had tricked him into the kiss was unforgettable.

What happened next was that Perv, his cock hard and throbbing, took his flick-knife and proceeded to hack off his own penis. Blood squirted everywhere. He knew he didn't want to do it. He knew it was me controlling him. As the blood pumped from his severed cock, he looked at me once more. Death would have been only minutes away. The Darkness let go of me. As I assessed what had happened, I chose to constrict his severed blood vessels and stop the bleeding. Letting him live. I did not want his death on my conscience despite what he had tried to do.

'I told you to stop,' I said coldly, 'but no! You had to keep going.'

'You fucking bitch,' he replied, 'you did this!' he said, as he looked at his withered cock laid on the ground; blood everywhere.

'Don't be silly, Michael, you did it to yourself. You did it out of shame for trying to rape me.'

'No, you did this witch. I'm going to tell everyone what you did. What I saw.'

'And they will think you are crazy.'

I heard my bus coming up the road, as it pulled up to let someone off, I had time to reach it. Fortunately, the arterial spray had not hit me as Michael had turned slightly before carving. Seems that the Darkness had it all covered.

The news the next day said that a man had been found seriously injured having mutilated himself as a result of drug abuse.

The police did come calling though. My mum had seen the news, and when the police knocked at the door, she cordially invited them in. Perhaps suspecting I had a hand in the reported events.

'Cathy,' she shouted up to my room, 'the police want a word with you.'

'Coming,' I shouted back. *I was ready.*

'Hello Cathy, my name is DC Lyons, and I'm investigating a strange incident that happened in the city park last night. Have you seen the news?'

'No, why?'

'Do you know Michael Purvis?'

'Yes, I do— in fact, I saw him last night.'

'Oh, you did?'

'Yes, I was at the bus stop, he came over to chat, he was acting a bit weird if I'm honest.'

'In what way was he acting weird?'

'I don't know, he just seemed a bit off. Maybe he'd taken something, I don't know, I'm no expert, am I?'

'And you're sure there is nothing else you can tell us?'

'No— is he in trouble for something?'

God damn, I'm good.

'Well, it's a bit awkward— you see for some reason he appears to have severely mutilated his genitalia.'

My mum immediately shot me a look.

'What? Why would he do that?' I asked.

'Well, this sounds even more strange, I know. But he seems very adamant that you made him do it.'

'Sorry—' I replied, giving yet another Oscar-winning look of surprise and disbelief at such a ridiculous accusation.

'And how exactly would she do that?' asked my mum.

'Yes, officer, how does he suppose I did that?'

'He says you cast some sort of spell on him,' he replied, seemingly caught between embarrassment and curiosity. *Maybe he was a believer!*

'Sorry— you are a qualified and educated individual, I assume,' interjected my mum. *Clearly now playing along with the whole charade.* 'I have never heard anything so ridiculous in all my life. Are we in an episode of *Tales of the Unexpected*? Or is this the twilight zone?' *Go, mum.*

'Look we chatted at the bus stop like I told you. He was being a bit weird as the bus pulled up, he walked towards the park. That's all I know.'

'So, you think he'd taken drugs, do you?'

'Well, like I said. I'm no expert, all I know is that he didn't seem quite himself; I really like Michael, is he going to be okay?'

'Well, his penis was too badly damaged and contaminated to be reattached.' *The officer let slip the extent of Michaels genital mutilation.*

'Oh, so he'll be Michelle, not Michael from now on then.' *Come on they gifted it to me.*

'CATHY!' chastised my mum.

'I don't think it's a laughing matter, Miss. He could have died,' replied DC Lyons, with a very disapproving look. *No sense of humour, some people!*

'Sorry.' I admonished myself.

'Oh, just one other thing, we found these at the scene, Michael says that they are yours and you were having sex with him in the park.'

The officer produced my torn pants in a plastic evidence bag. *Fucker! Bet he sniffed them too. He looks the type.*

'Are they yours he asked, we can verify with DNA tests if we need to.' The officer looked like he had just cracked a significant case.

My next Oscar comes for inprov.

Without missing a beat, without the slightest hesitation.

'Look, it's embarrassing, and I didn't want to discuss it in front of my mum. I also didn't want to further embarrass Michael or get him in trouble. He was going to force himself on me. He cut off my pants with his flick-knife. Aren't they illegal by the way? Anyway, he couldn't get it up. No matter what he tried, he couldn't get hard. I heard the bus coming up the road, while he was distracted, I made my escape, leaving him with his knife and limp dick in hand.'

The officer seemed a little uncomfortable with my risqué and adult-like explanation.

'Why didn't you call the police and report it?'

'Look, Michael is okay. I do quite like him. If he had taken drugs, then maybe he was acting under their influence. He didn't actually hurt me or rape me so why bother? Rapists rarely get prosecuted, and I'm the one who ends up on trial as the accuser. And we did have a bit of a kiss. So, I would be forced to put up with them saying; *she was asking for it*. It's not worth the grief if I'm honest.'

'Don't believe all you read in the papers, Miss. We take sex crimes very seriously.'

'Well, that's good to hear PC Lyons.'

'Err— It's DC Lyons.' *I knew that.*

'Oh— Sorry.'

'How old are you Cathy?'

'I'm fourteen, I'm still a virgin. Michael suspected this. He said he'd *pop my cherry* and that he'd be gentle.'

'Isn't Michael eighteen?' asked my mum.

'Yes, well, almost I think,' I replied. *What a tag team.*

'Well then that is statutory rape isn't it officer?' asserted my mum.

'Yes, it is, or would have been had he managed to perform.'

'Well, it is at the least sexual assault of a minor.' Continued my mum. 'and then there is the issue of carrying an offensive weapon with intent.' *Go mum the barrister.*

'Look— let us decide what charges are appropriate.'

'So why are you harassing my daughter over a rapist with an offensive weapon who self-harmed because he was on drugs?' *He doesn't have an offensive weapon now— I will keep that one to myself.*

'I'm sorry to have bothered you both, we have to follow these things up. I hope you understand?'

'What? — understand that you investigate accusations of witchcraft in the twentieth century!' scoffed my mum, 'The Witchcraft Act of 1735 was repealed in 1951, so you couldn't charge her even if she were a witch.' *Oh, God— Too far, mum.*

'You seem very well-informed madam, on such a spurious piece of legislation.'

'It's my hobby, A guilty pleasure. I work at the library and love history, particularly the dark-ages. But we don't live in the dark-ages anymore do we officer. Oh— and it wasn't a spurious piece of legislation if you were unfortunate enough to be accused of witchcraft. But as we both know, officer— Witches don't exist. Do they?' *excellent recovery there, mum.*

The officer was beaten.

'Well, thanks again for your time, ladies,' he replied apologetically.

As mum closed the door, she turned to me, I was sloping off upstairs.

'Back here, lady— NOW!'

'What?'

'I assume you did make him chop his penis off?'

'Well technically it was the Darkness actually— but he was going to rape me, and then I think he was going to kill me.'

'Oh!'

'Oh, Indeed, mum.'

'That sort of magic is extremely dark Cathy, it is forbidden.'

'Tell that to the Darkness! He was driving.'

'I thought you had that under control?'

'Mum, Michael was going to rape and murder me! It was self-defence. He is alive, but he won't be raping anyone again. You told me that the Darkness will not allow anyone to harm me. It was him not me who did that to Michael!'

It turns out that taking a man's penis leaves him full of hate and vengeance. *I guess it figures*. Michael had clearly planned his revenge quite carefully. Credit where it's due.

A month or so after his self-administered penectomy. Michael had clearly been watching our movements. He knocked at our door. My mum was out with my sister. As I opened the door, it was too late. He struck me hard. When I woke, I was tied to a chair in our kitchen.

'Hey— Cathy.'

'Hey— Michelle,' I said with a grin. *I knew it would rile him, but I said it anyway.*

'You won't be laughing when I have done with you. You fucking witch bitch.'

'What do you intend to do, you can't rape me! Not unless that is— you brought a strap-on with you.'

I recognise there is both a time and a place for levity and sarcasm. *Maybe this wasn't it.* Fuck it*! I knew something he didn't.*

'I am going to cut off your tits— then I'm going to shove this up your tight little virgin snatch and fuck up your womb. Then you won't be a woman, just as I'm no longer a man. Thanks to you!'

'Wow— Michael that is actually a well thought out revenge scenario for such a fucktard.'

'I Know.'

'What? — you know you're a fucktard?'

'Keep it up, bitch, and I might even take an eye.'

'Yeah, I can keep it up— unlike you.' *What the hell in for a penny in for a pound as they say.*

Michael was now raging. Ready to start carving at any moment.

'You have a dirty little mouth, Cathy. I thought you were a nice girl.'

'I am a nice girl Michael. I don't talk like this to my family and friends— No! I save it for idiots like you. Bullies like Thomas Crossland and Grace Haigh.'

'I knew it! I knew you'd done that to Thomas.'

'Well, go to the top of the class Perv. Sherlock Investigates!'

'You are a witch.'

'Yes, Michael, I am. But I'm much more than that. I am protected from harm by the devil himself. He did this to you. Because I was scared and in danger. But he's not here now. Because I'm not frightened of you, and I'm not in danger.

'You think? What do you think this is?' Asked Michael waving his blade in my face. 'You are in danger, you evil bitch, you're just too stupid to know it.'

'That's a big old zombie knife you have there Perv. Watch you don't cut yourself. You know what happened the last time you pulled a knife on me.'

'You can't fucking help it can you? You think you're so fucking funny.'

'What's with the snide Ray-Ban's Michelle? Do you think you look cool?'

'They're so that you can't look me in the eye, bitch. I'm not fucking stupid.'

'Well, who are you fucking then?'

'I'm going to fuck you— with this!' he replied as he pressed the tip of the knife to my throat.

'Wow, you have given it some thought, haven't you?'

'You seem calm Cathy. For someone about to get sliced and diced, that is.'

'Yeah well, you see the thing you missed bright spark is that once I swallowed your blood. I can actually control you at will and at any time as long as you are within range. I don't need eye contact.'

His face changed. The cocky, *no pun intended*, look on his face changed instantly to one of horror.

'Nice try— but you're bluffing,' he replied with very little conviction.

'Really?'

As I spoke, I took control once more. He was now frozen to the spot. A look of panic registering as the twelve-inch zombie knife in his hand moved toward his neck. It now rested with the razor-sharp edge across his throat. The hilt resting to the right of and just below his Adams-apple. His elbow parallel to his shoulder. His left hand removed his sunglasses.

'Perfect,' I said.

Try as he might, he could not break free of my grasp.

'Okay, Okay, you win,' he pleaded.

I smiled coldly. *This was me, not the Darkness. The Darkness had no hand in this. Though he was doubtless watching his prodigy, coming of age.*

'What am I to do with you, Michelle?'

'Let me go, you will never see me again, I swear.'

'You couldn't leave it alone, could you? I let you live when the Darkness wanted you dead, but no. I showed you compassion even after you'd attempted to rape me and who knows what else you'd intended?'

'You chopped my fucking cock off. What did you expect?'

'No, you chopped it off! Just as you're going to cut your own throat in front of me now!'

'Please I beg you, don't do it, I know you are a good person Cathy. Please, you're not a murderer.'

'I gave you a chance. I gave Thomas a chance. Seems you boys don't know when to call it a day. You come to my home looking to mutilate me. You think I can let that slide, do you?'

'You're not a murderer Cathy, please I beg you.'

Michael had actually started to cry.

'You know what Michael—

'What?'

'I would have more respect if you had said to me; *fuck you witch*— *kill me then*— This begging and crying makes me hate you even more. You are a coward and a bully. I have no time for either— If I let you live, next time you come for me, you will just kill me outright. If you watch the movies, Michael, you'll know it never ends well when the villain insists on keeping their nemesis alive just to toy with them. No, you will try again because you are a coward— Oh, and It's not murder, its self-defence. No! — it's suicide.'

'Cathy— please you can't kill me.'

'Michael— let me tell you a secret— I killed my own father! A man I loved and respected very much— I will give no quarter to you!'

Hearing those words, Michael's face acknowledged his fate.

'See you in hell— Witch!' he hissed.

'You'd better hope not Michael!'

Michaels right arm pulled the blade slowly and deliberately across his throat, the knife was sharp and the pressure firm, his windpipe was severed, blood ran into his lungs as he gurgled. Foaming blood was blown back through his nose and mouth. A truly horrendous death. I sat and watched; dangerously void of any compassion. I would have felt worse had I accidentally killed a spider, than I did seeing this dickless idiot drown in his own blood. It did, however, make me realise that I had the capability to be evil and sadistic, without any encouragement from the Darkness. That thought did unsettle me. I felt no compassion, no sorrow, no sadness, no remorse— just a tinge of pity for poor dickless Michael. I should have let him die the first time. *My mistake. Lesson learnt.*

Michael hit the floor with a thud. Dead! Good!

I was found by my mum, an hour or so later. The police were called.

The scene was a bloody mess. Forensic teams worked tirelessly gathering the evidence, pictures of blood spatter patterns seemed to show that Michael had indeed; unaided by me, cut his own throat.

Good old DC Lyons interviewed me at the police station with my mum present. I told them Michael had felt so ashamed and embarrassed at not being able to get it up. So ashamed in fact, that he had tried to rape me; he had decided that, as he was no longer a man, something he seemed to blame me for; that he would punish me by making me watch him kill himself. He said that he wanted me to have nightmares for the rest of my life. *No such luck. They seemed to believe me.*

The questioning came to a close, and the tape recorder was switched off.

'No more accusations of witchcraft then, Officer?' asked my Mum.

DC Lyons paused.

For some bizarre reason, mum appeared to be taunting him. Maybe that's where I get it from?

'No Mrs Heely, not today,' he replied drolly.

Lyons shuffled his papers that mum had just signed. He then cast a look in my direction.

Sorry but I just couldn't resist.

I, for the briefest moment. For the mere blink of an eye— let him see. He couldn't entirely be sure. Maybe it was the light playing tricks. I smiled with a knowing smile. Knowing it had unnerved him just enough. Knowing he could do or say nothing about what he saw for fear of ridicule.

Mum shook his hand as we readied ourselves to leave. He reached out to shake my hand too.

'Take care, Cathy. Try and stay out of trouble.' *What a condescending prick.*

'You don't need to worry about me, PC Lyons. I can take care of myself,' I replied with a cheeky smile. *He didn't correct me as to his rank— he knew I was yanking his chain. I knew we would meet again. I think I became an off-book, personal project for him. I do so enjoy a battle of wits. Shame he'd come to the fight unarmed.*

DC Lyons would also spend the afternoon in the toilet with a dreadful case of the squirts.

Chapter 10
How the Tables Turned

Okay, so I entered puberty at age ten, my body underwent rapid change by twelve years of age I was one of only three or four girls in my year who had developed a good set of boobs.

This meant I went from being the witch that everyone avoided, to being one of the most sought-after girls in my year.

Seems a pair of tits have powers similar to the others that I possessed. *No hiding them though.*

Also, with my boobs came hormonally driven mood swings and a sexual yearning that was strong.

So anyway, I experimented with masturbation, I let some of the better-looking boys give me *digital stimulation* as I believe is the politically correct phrase for getting fingered. I would give the odd hand job in return. I managed to hold on to my virginity until I was sixteen.

A new boy named Danny had started sixth-form. He was a bit of a rocker, ruggedly good looking a bit of a Scott Eastwood; with his own rock band, he being the drummer. All the girls wanted him. He though— only had eyes for me.

He wasn't a virgin. What he unleashed on our first night together though! — Shook his world. I doubt — No, in fact, I know that try as he may; he will never encounter sex like he had with me. After that, I just wanted sex all the time. No tender lovemaking, just raw, lust-filled and passionate sex. I had seemingly become a nymphomaniac almost overnight, and my appetite was almost insatiable. I didn't mind if it was girl on girl, boy on girl or any combination thereof.

My powers enable me to control some bodily functions; I can manage pain for short durations. However, sexually, I had a trick or two that was good for me and for the boys; or girls for that matter; always leaving them begging for more.

I can also control my lover's metabolism enough to act like Viagra; giving them immense staying power.

From my studies, it appears that my sexual urges are all part of my development as a witch; the chemical and hormonal releases caused by such activity grows my powers. Once these have peaked my desire subsides somewhat. Though I am, I have to admit, pretty horny most of the time.

It was not until I reached my early twenties. Well, in fact, as predicted by my mum at the age of twenty-one; that it all settled down to a more manageable level.

So firstly, I was seen as a bit of a freak the little witch! Then I got boobs, and the boys all loved me. The other girls hated me. I ended up labelled a dirty slut. Seems you just can't win. You can please all of the people some of the time, some of the people all of the time, but never all of the people all of the time; to slightly bastardise Abraham Lincolns quote.

Well, who cares? Life is not a popularity contest; I had a couple of good girlfriends and one or two boys who were reliable mates and friends with benefits.

My life eventually settled down to some level of normality. I loved my art and had sold some pieces. I had a job at a small independent printer and specialist publisher. I even had a serious boyfriend.

Chapter 11
Me and My Man

I had just finished the Sixth form, it was 2001. I had made a few new friends. I was past all the witch related jibes and felt more emotionally and spiritually settled than I had for a while.

This was at odds with the fact I was now eighteen— the sum of six, six, six as my mum had pointed out would be my most testing year. Maybe that was yet to come. Perhaps it wasn't. Maybe the Darkness had given up on me. I hoped.

We— I say we— My friends were going out for the end of college drinks. I didn't drink for obvious reasons. Can you imagine the carnage I would likely leave in my wake, was I to have an alcohol-induced temper tantrum?

My friends convinced me to come along at least for the first part of the night. They were starting off in Delaney's bar before later hitting the clubs.

I decided I would make an effort. I might feel settled, but I still felt horny. I had the perfect outfit. A figure-hugging black number. Tastefully short. My hair in ringlets falling just below my shoulders.

This was a contrast to my daily attire. I liked jeans, T-shirts and trainers, my hair tied back and no makeup. I tended to attract less attention that way.

I did, however— as they say— *Scrub up well*. I was blessed with an hourglass figure. I say blessed. I was able to control my own metabolism somewhat and my bodies fat distribution. Often described as curvaceous and voluptuous, I was as they say— built for fun.

I have, on many occasions, walked into bars, where almost everyone has stopped to look. Very empowering, I must say. If you've got it— flaunt it! This though, is tempered somewhat by the fact that I am inherently quite shy and do not like being the centre of attention. My sexual allure though suited my hormonally or witch driven need to quench my sexual thirsts. I must have seemed like a Jekyll and Hyde— one minute I don't even want to make eye contact the next I'm tearing off my clothes— extraordinary times indeed.

We all hooked up as planned at 7:30p.m. I was last to arrive. No not so that I could make a grand entrance. Well, maybe a little.

Jenny, Clare and Fran were sat at a table halfway down the main bar area. I got the usual looks. The odd comment as I did the catwalk. One guy at the bar caught my eye. *Cute!*

The girls had my soda and lime waiting for me. They not being quite so reserved all had some vodka-based alcopop.

The conversation was typical. We were all selecting from the bar's clientele who we would or wouldn't do! We were all single at the time. I had slept with Jenny on a couple of occasions, but the other two were unaware. Jenny was sweet. She did like men. I was an exception. She and I did have a close friendship though, and she had brought a calmness to my life. We did hang out quite a lot. She was also doing art, and like me, she loved the natural world.

Jenny and I would often take picnic's to local beauty spots; take our sketchbooks and just enjoy what we had. We would talk for hours, and I trusted her. Few people gain that accolade with me. But Jenny was like the sister I should have had.

I had toyed with confiding in her. But as yet, I hadn't done so. The truth would be a burden. It may also put her in harm's way. Knowing the truth might complicate things too. What would be gained by her knowing? There was also the real possibility that the truth may well scare her away. I think it would me.

'That guy at the bar— the cute one— he can't take his eyes off you, Cathy,' said Jenny.

'Yeah, I clocked him when I came in— I definitely would,' I laughed.

'Yeah me too,' replied Jenny.

By now Clare and Fran had joined in.

'I'd have his babies— no question,' said Clare.

'I don't think he has any interest in any of us girls. He seems almost hypnotised by our Cathy,' said Fran.

'Yeah, she is looking hot tonight,' replied Jenny, 'I'd even consider doing her myself,' she continued with a sly wink that only I saw.

Clare and Fran looked at Jenny with a look of moderate disapproval— Eww — lezza,' they joked.

'So, ladies, what are your plans now that we've finished college?' I asked.

'I think I will try and sell my work independently and I'm also considering illustrating children's books. I don't want to do a job I hate just to get by,' replied Jenny.

'Yeah, it must be nice if you can land a job you love. Most people don't and generally, if you do something you like the pay is usually rubbish,' commented Fran.

'The other problem is that if you love doing something and then make a career out of it, you might end up hating that too,' I said. 'What about you, Clare?'

'I don't know— maybe just find a rich hunk to take care of me.'

'Trust you, Clare.'

'Well she has a point,' joked Fran, 'be a kept woman— I could do that.'

'I thought we were all independent women— you've misled me all this time,' I replied.

'Yes, but honestly who in the world actually wants to work if they don't have to?' Said Clare.

'Anyway, Mrs judgemental— what are your plans?' asked Fran.

'Well this day— end of college— seems to have come out of the blue— it's taken me by surprise how quickly the time has flown. You lot have been the best.'

'Yes, we know— so answer the question,' said Jenny.

'Well, I would like to also sell my work. I do so enjoy being at one with nature and capturing it in all its beauty. I will see which direction fate takes me— maybe the cute guy at the bar is loaded,' I replied.

'Yeah, and with a big dick too,' said Clare.

'Clare, you're filthy,' I admonished.

'Says you who seems to have fucked her way through all the best guys in college,' replied Clare with a smile.

'I don't know what you mean,' I replied, smiling back at Clare.

'You're fucking rampant Cathy,' said Fran.

'I do enjoy sex, but then you all know that already— we've been mates for a good two years now.'

'Yeah, we just got to pick up the spent left-overs after you'd shagged them to death,' noted Jenny.

'I've always found you a bit of a conundrum Cathy,' started Fran, 'you dress like a tomboy most of the time in college. You get on with your work, keep your head down and seem almost shy. We struggle to get you out of the house at times— Then you come out looking like some Hollywood superstar full of confidence, oozing sexuality and sensuality—'

'I am complicated; it's true. A better friend I challenge you to find though.'

'I agree Cathy. I would trust you with my life,' said Jenny.

'If I call you my friend then unless you fuck me over, I would die for any one of you. Trust, loyalty, love and compassion girls— that should be everyone's code. I love you all.'

'Whoa, I'm starting to fill up here,' said Fran.

'Yeah me too, you soppy cow,' said Clare.

'I'm just saying— it will be strange not seeing you all every day— I will miss you all.'

The time whizzed by, and it was 9:30pm when Clare announced it was time to head to Rebecca's a popular club further uptown.

'We'll call in for a swift one at Jesters and then hit Becca's.' said Clare authoritatively.

'Yeah— you girls get off. I might go and pull cute guy at the bar. I'll give you the lowdown next time I see you.'

'Yeah, I bet— If he fancies a threesome let me know,' Said Jenny, 'I'll ditch these two losers.'

'Oi— Lezza— who you calling losers?' Joked Fran as they all headed out of the door.

I decided to have a single shot for the road. Maybe just maybe cute guy might make a move. I didn't have an issue making the first move, but I wanted him to work for it, if that's what he wanted.

'I'll have a whiskey please,' I said to the barmaid.

'Single?'

'Yes— I am. Why? do you want my number?' I joked. *She was cute too.*

She just gave me a cheeky smile.

'What the hell I'll have a double,' I replied. Looking to catch cute guy's eye.

'Let me get that,' offered cute guy.

'That's very kind of you. Thanks.'

He sidled over to me from where he was stood.

'Hi— I'm Paul,' he said.

'Cathy,' I replied.

'This isn't me being crass— but you are stunning— breathtakingly stunning in fact.'

Shucks. Now I feel all self-conscious. NOT! It would be so easy to reply, 'yes I know' but I really do find the whole compliment thing a little awkward.

'You're pretty good looking yourself, Mister,' I replied, 'So, what's your story, Paul?'

Paul was five-feet nine-ish. He was handsome, fit body. Not ripped by any stretch but well proportioned. Medium length black hair. Styled.

It's difficult sometimes. I don't like Smalltalk, but I can be very direct and maybe a little crude at times. Some men find that off-putting— others really get off on it. I have found few men who really like the woman taking control. It's okay for a kick. But not as a regular thing. They feel intimidated by a strong and confident woman; in my experience at least.

So, I was forever playing the game of testing the water to see which camp they fell in; so that I could hopefully be more myself.

'I'm a photographer,' he started.

'Glamour?'

'No actually— why are you a glamour model?'

'Touché— '

'I do a lot of commercial photography, corporate and the like. I do portraits, but it's all a bit cheesy.'

'That's cool. I'm an artist. I've just finished college, in fact, this was our end of school bash. But I don't drink. In fact, I don't socialise much outside of the college environment. Actually, now I think about it— I suppose this will be a turning point for me.'

I hadn't considered this really. I had settled well into the college routine. It gave me access to virile young males without any need for complicated relationships.

'I don't wish to speak out of turn but why would someone with so much to offer hide away? You don't seem the shy type either so it can't be that'

'I don't hide away as you put it, socialising and fitting in just isn't a priority for me. Equally I don't walk around looking like this all the time either.'

'You can't hide that beauty. You'd have to walk around with a bag on your head.'

'Look I used to get teased at school, I guess kids pick up when there is something a little different about you and I do get very self-conscious as a result.'

'Yeah, I suppose kids can be cruel.'

'Yes, and it can damage you for life Paul.'

'Look, I do fancy you. I guess the fact I haven't been able to take my eyes off you for the past two hours made that fairly obvious.'

'Really? — I hadn't noticed,' I said with a grin.

'So, look— there is a new all-night bistro bar in town. Let's go get a snack and have a chat. I'd love to get to know you, Cathy. I know its cheesy— but you're not like the other girls. I'm hooked. Sorry but if you say no I'll just stalk you.'

'You'd not rather just take me back to your place then.'

Paul froze momentarily as he processed my remark.

'How do I even answer that? If I say no, then you'd ask why? Am I not your type? I'd also be lying. But if that's what you want. Surely, we can save it until later. I just want to get to know you at least a little bit before we do the dirty deed.'

Well, that was certainly not typical. Paul did seem a little different to my usual pick-up.

'Okay— I'm good with that.'

'Come on then, let's get out of here.'

We grabbed a cab to the bistro bar and found a seat away from the bar. The place had a Mexican theme and made an excellent tapas type of snack selection. I do love my food, so we ordered and started our session of getting to know you.

'So now you have finished college, what are your plans?'

'Well, I'd really like to draw. I am fortunate to have great natural ability; and I'd love to have an exhibition.'

'Hey— I know people who can showcase your stuff if it really is that good.'

'You doubt me do you, Paul?' I said with a grin.

'No, but as with many things, people sometimes have an unrealistic view of their talents. You only have to watch the X-factor to know that.'

'Trust me, I am not one of those people.'

'What do you like to draw?'

'Nature in all its glory.'

'Have you travelled?'

'No, I have a condition that makes that difficult.'

'What condition would that be? — if that's not me getting too personal too soon.'

'I suffer from acute anxiety.'

'What? — you seem too confident to suffer from anxiety.'

'Yeah, who knew— right? You've known me for an hour, Paul and you're psychoanalysing me already. What makes you such an expert?'

'I'm just shocked to hear that, no offence intended— What do you get anxious about?'

'Well, it's complicated but basically; that I will succumb to evil dark forces and bring about the apocalypse!'

'Okay—sorry I asked—so, moving on. I assume you don't have a boyfriend?'

'No, I don't— but never assume anything, Paul.'

'How come you haven't been snapped up. You must have your choice of would-be suitors?'

'Well perhaps I just choose not to be snapped up.'

'So, you're not looking for a serious relationship?' asked Paul, seeming a little deflated at my response.

'Let's just say that I have issues with trust, Paul.'

'So, you've been let down badly in the past?'

'You can't even begin to imagine.'

'It would be a shame if you let your past dictate your future, we all make mistakes.'

'It's only a mistake if you don't learn from it. Otherwise, it's a lesson. I have learned my lessons the hard way. Believe me. You seem a genuinely lovely guy Paul. But you would let me down. Everyone does in the end— and then— '

'And then— what?'

'You've heard the term hell hath no fury like a woman scorned?'

'You're badass, are you.'

'More than you will ever know Paul.'

'Well if I let you down, I would deserve everything you'd do to me.'

'You say that now.'

'I mean it. I am drawn to you Cathy in a way I have never felt before.'

'I have to say you make a refreshing change. Maybe that's because I usually go for certain types.'

'So, am I not your type?'

'I'm still trying to decide.'

'So why did you get teased so badly at school?'

'Well don't laugh—but I looked a little bit like Wednesday Adams— complete with resting bitch face.'

Paul laughed— 'I bet they don't think that now.'

'They used to call me witch— Carrie and all the other names that I'm sure you can guess.'

'Well your eyes and that raven hair says princess of Darkness to me.'

'You think so do you? — I can go off people you know.'

'I mean it as a compliment Cathy— you have an air of mystery and a dark allure it is such a turn on.'

'Well careful what you wish for Paul.'

'So, have you decided if I'm your type yet?'

'I'm still working on that. I avoid relationships Paul. If I don't let people in, then I can't get hurt.'

'But if you don't let people in, you will never know love Cathy. Do you want to go through life never having loved or being loved?'

'You have a point Paul. And no, I don't want to go through life not knowing love. Seriously though if I loved it would be full on. Unconditional love. But if I was betrayed, I fear the consequences would be catastrophic.'

'Break-ups are never easy Cathy.'

'I'm not talking about a relationship that fizzles out Paul— I am talking about betrayal and that is what holds me back.'

'Cathy, I swear on my life; I would never let you down in that way. It is not in my nature.'

'I wonder how many people say that— marriage vows are a good example of commitment and how many people go on to have affairs?'

'I wish you would give me a chance to prove you wrong Cathy. I always thought love at first sight was a myth— now I'm not so sure.'

'That's a great line Paul. But you're getting laid tonight so no need to try too hard.'

'I am serious Cathy. I have never in my life felt like this.'

Okay, so now I am a little outside my comfort zone. I do like him— A lot— maybe I even feel the same way about him.

'Okay— slow it down a little— that's a little overwhelming Paul. But I appreciate what you're saying, and I do like you— but let's take a breather.'

Subject changed; we continued to talk, and then we talked some more. It was 2:00a.m, and we were still chatting. The streets were getting busier as people headed out from the clubs. A couple of guys entered the Bistro bar and order tequila shots. They were on their way to being drunk. But not quite there yet.

Clearly, though they were drunk enough to think they were funny in a slightly confrontational way.

'Fuck— you are gorgeous,' said the larger of the two men.

These were not tattooed yobs. They were well dressed. Designer clothes and expensive watches. I hated these spoilt city types more than the tattooed hard cases. In fact, some of the nicest people I know are covered in tattoos.

'Thanks— but I'm out of your league,' I replied without hesitation. *Sorry! And this is why I can't be trusted out.*

'What the fuck did you just say to me? Do you know who I am?'

'I suppose it will further hurt your feelings and bruise your ego if I say no— but no, I don't know who you are, other than an irritating wanker. Are you a local celebrity or something?'

Paul was momentarily speechless. I'd just told him I suffered from acute anxiety.

'What the fuck did you call me?'

'An irritating wanker— are you deaf as well?'

'— how about I beat the shit out of your mute pussy boyfriend over there and then maybe show you what it's like to have a real man.'

'Todd mate leave it. She's just winding you up pal.' Interjected Todd's mate, in an effort to calm the situation.

Too late I am as they say— triggered!

'Yeah— listen to your boyfriend, Todd.'

'You saying I'm Gay?'

'No actually— because of all the gay guys I know— none of them would act like such arseholes.'

'I'm going to slap that smug look off your face bitch.'

'How about you fuck off before you get hurt Todd.'

Paul grabbed my arm.

'Leave it, Cathy. They're not worth it.'

'Bullies are always worth it, Paul.'

'Look, fellas— we don't want any trouble, she's feeling a bit emotional, she's just finished college. It's just a bit of silly banter,' Interjected Paul, in an attempt to diffuse— well to diffuse me.

'Shut it! You fucking pussy,' replied Todd.

'Listen— you need to calm down— you're going to burst a blood vessel,' I said as I looked him in the eye.

Some of the customers in the bar were by now clearing the way for what looked like an ensuing scrap. Todd's mate was at his shoulder ready to back up his pal; just in case a woman and her pussy boyfriend were too much for him to handle.

I got up to confront him. Face to face. Toe to toe. *Just how I liked it*. Paul jumped to his feet, ready for it all kicking off.

'You've got some fucking balls— I'll give you that,' said Todd.

'Yeah— I've got balls and you and your mate are a pair of tits, quite ironic really.'

'So, what you gonna do, bitch.'

'I'm still thinking about it— I will give you the chance to turn around and walk out of the bar. If not— well I can't be held responsible, can I?'

'You talk the fucking talk. Can you walk the walk? Your big mouth is all you've got,' replied Todd as he stared intently into my eyes.

'Is it?' I replied as I let the Darkness say hello.

Suddenly Todd clutched his chest. Seconds later, he was on the floor.

'Someone call an ambulance I think he's having a heart attack,' I shouted.

I heard someone in the crowd say; 'serves him right the prick. He's given himself a heart attack.' *Not quite. But close enough— He'll live.*

His mate looked at me as if it were somehow my fault. *As if!*

'You want some, do you?' I snarled.

Paul grabbed my arm and ushered me out of the bar; to a round of applause from some of the customers.

'Fucking hell Cathy. You're fucking mental. What would you have done had he not had a heart attack? I'd got your back, but it wouldn't have been pretty.'

'I can take care of myself.'

'What? Do you do martial arts? Are you some secret cage fighter or a fucking Ninja?'

'No, I have the prince of Darkness watching my back.'

'Look I said sorry for the comment, are you going to hold it against me forever?'

'Oh, chill out Paul— I'm only messing.'

'I've never seen anything like that before. You are fucking crazy. I thought you said you suffer from anxiety for fuck's sake?'

'You still wanna be friends?'

'Yes, I do— absolutely. It'll take more than that to scare me off.'

'Okay so is it back to yours then, that's made me quite horny?'

'You know what Cathy. Much as I would love to. Let's have another date, let's break this cycle you seem to be in. Believe me, I'll be getting home and doing some serious DIY, but let's slow it down. You crazy fuck.'

Wow, I never had. Not once. Ever. Been turned down. It felt strange.

'What about a kiss at least?'

'Sure— '

We kissed. WOW! So hard not to drop to the floor and do it right there in the street.

'Fuck— I'm almost tempted now,' said Paul, as he took stock.

Go on— you know you want to.'

'I do— but No! Can I walk you home?'

'No, I'm a taxi ride away. What about you?'

'Oh— just a ten-minute walk. Maybe I'll have calmed down by the time I get home.'

'Best swap numbers then— you can walk me to the taxi rank.'

'Sure— here is my business card.'

'Great— I'll text you then you'll have mine.'

'Cool.'

'You will call me, won't you?'

'No danger.'

As we arrived at the taxi rank, we kissed briefly.

'See you then,' I said with a smile.

Chapter 12
Roses are Red Violence is too.

Paul and I met again just two days later. We went for lunch. We chatted for hours. It seemed so easy and so natural. To be fair, I had even pushed thoughts of sex to the back of my mind. Not completely mind you, and I was determined I'd bed him today. But it was not my primary thought at least.

'Did you see the newspaper about that guy we had the run-in with?'

'No— what did it say?'

'It said witnesses had confirmed he was having a verbal altercation with a young woman and that he seemingly got so worked up that he had a heart attack.'

'Serves him right.'

'Apparently, it was quite serious and will affect him for the rest of his life. He is the son of some millionaire property developer. Absolutely loaded by all accounts.'

'All that money won't do him much good now will it?'

'I guess not. I still can't believe it. You just seemed to switch to psycho bitch.'

'Look when you get picked on generally you develop coping mechanisms or perhaps defence mechanisms, mine are many but primarily I resort to sarcasm and inappropriate humour.'

'You went toe to toe with that guy. He was not going to back down.'

'Neither was I. I hate bullies and will never back down to one; I don't care how big they are.'

'If he hadn't had the heart attack, he would have hit you.'

'No, he wouldn't.'

'He would have.'

'Look Paul, enough about me, we never got to talk much about you. You're fit, so why aren't you snapped up, as you so eloquently put it?'

'I've had a couple of serious girlfriends. But none really did it for me. I knew they weren't really hitting the spot, so no point dragging things on; only to make the hurt worse when I finally end it.'

'That's fair, I guess. If you feel it's not a goer, then why force it or string them along.'

'Exactly.'

'How old are you, Paul?'

'Twenty-three.'

'So, do you want children?'

He paused and looked a little uncomfortable.

'Paul, I'm not asking you to father my children; it's just a bit of getting to know you chit chat.'

'It's not that— I'm not really into the whole kid's scene if I'm honest.'

'Well just so that you know, and so you can shine me on if it's an issue before we get too serious. I can't have children.'

'Listen— it's not an issue. Would you want them if you could though?'

'To be honest — No!'

'Okay— that's a major hurdle kicked into touch,' replied Paul, almost triumphantly.

'Are there any other potential showstoppers that you can think of?'

'Nope— that's me done,' replied Paul with a smile.

'Well let me be honest Paul there is something which you need to know.'

'Oh— what might that be?'

'Well, it might seem like a dream come true. But it's not.'

'What might?'

Well, I suppose I could be best described as a nymphomaniac.'

'Wow— really not a problem,' replied Paul, his eyes widening with anticipation and a massive grin appearing on his face.

'That's what they all say. You see most men would love to meet a nympho. It is the stuff of dreams. The truth is few men have either the stamina or for that matter the libido. They just think they do. A woman with an insatiable sex drive will outstrip any man; even if he considers he too has an unquenchable sexual thirst.'

'You're kidding, right.'

'Nope. It's all fun and games for the first week or two.'

'No way— I can't see me ever saying no to you.'

'Seriously it might be an issue for you.'

'So, what happens if I can't keep up— you kick me into touch and find some other Joe, or do you have an affair. What?'

'I don't know— I've never felt like this about anyone before. So yes, I kick them into touch, or rather they call it a day. If I committed to you Paul, then I would have to manage my urges. And believe me, it's not easy to do. I would never cheat. I am reliably informed that it's hormonal and will pass or at least settle down once I reach twenty-one.'

'So, for three years, you will pretty much fuck me to death.'

'Something like that.'

'Well— I guess I will have to take one for the team,' replied Paul confidently.

'Okay, then.'

'Look you are stunning; you have a smouldering sensuality and a body—'

'— built for fun, I know.'

'So, what you are saying is that for three years I will need to nail you on-demand? I just can't ever see that being a problem.'

'Do you not feel a little intimidated by it?'

'I'd be lying if I said no— I might prove to be a flop.'

'I hope not.'

'Yeah, a flop— not floppy. I'm rock hard right now, to be honest.'

'Back to your place then.'

'Let's do it.' *I told you I'd bed him today.*

We arrived at Pauls apartment. It was quite impressive. Business must be good.

We made it to the bedroom. Just.

A flop he most certainly was not. I let loose with all my tricks. His face was a picture. Paul was attentive, passionate and tender. I kept him going for three whole hours without a break.

Both sweaty and breathless, we eventually lay side by side. He pulled me close. I'd typically get up and leave at this point. Usually never to see the spent lover again. But this did feel different somehow.

'That was something else,' said Paul as he caught his breath.

'I told you— I'm only just getting warmed up,' I joked.

I did feel satisfied, something I rarely felt.

'You're joking, right?'

'Maybe—' I teased.

'Fuck— I hope you're jesting.'

'What happened to taking one for the team. I need this three times a day every fucking day.'

'Really?'

'Well, I might be laying it on a little thick.'

'You have incredible pelvic floor control.'

'That's not what that is— but I'm glad you like it.'

Both spent and both relaxed and content we drifted off to sleep.

Waking some hours later.

'Want to go again?' I asked.

'In the words of Nickelback— if the questions sex— then the answers yes— or something like that,' Paul replied.

'That's ma boy.'

Our relationship really blossomed. I was getting out more. The Darkness seemed a distant memory. Paul had the idea that we join forces artistically and that he photographs a scene. I also, at the same time, sketch the same scene. We then combine the works for visual impact as a comparison between our two crafts.

It was working well, we had our work featured in some local galleries, and we were selling pieces almost as quickly as we could produce them.

Two years into our relationship Paul Proposed. I accepted. No date was set.

It was a lovely summers day, and we had gone to a local stately home to do some pieces and to chill and enjoy the weather. Paul had gone to fetch Ice-creams I sat taking in the scenery.

'Cathy is that you?' said a voice from my left.

I turned to see James, one of Thomas Crossland's old gang of two.'

'Wow look at you,' he continued.

'Oh, Hi James— what brings you here?'

'What too good for me, is it?'

'Jim, that's not what I meant, and you know it. Why are you looking to start trouble?'

'Who knew you'd turn out to be so fit. The little witch turned out alright.'

'Don't start with all the witch shit, Jim— how old are we?'

'Fuck you are a fine piece of pussy Cathy.'

At this point, Paul returned with our ice-creams.

'Everything okay, Cathy?' asked Paul seeing that I looked somewhat miffed.

'Fine— just someone I know from school who doesn't seem to have grown up.'

'Is he bothering you?'

'No, I'm not bothering her. I was just saying how much she's changed since the little witch I knew from School— she's certainly worth one.'

'Listen, mate, why don't you just move on,' suggested Paul in a calm but firm, manner.

'Or else what? And I ain't your fucking mate!'

Now, Jim, the sycophantic little mate of Thomas, had grown up and filled out. He did have tattoos, and he did look like trouble.

I stood up from the blanket where I was sat.

'Look Jim— take a hike will you.'

'Or what? You'll make me go blind like you did with Tommy.'

'Just Fuck off, Jim.'

'Go on, you fucking witch. I fucking dare you.'

'To do what exactly?'

'To strike me down— or make me piss my pants maybe.'

'It's not my fault Tommy was a gutless little bully. A bit like you.'

'I'll show you, bully. Bitch!'

'I will only ask you once more Jim or whoever the fuck you are. Leave us be,' said Paul forcefully.

'She doesn't need you pal. This one can take care of herself, can't you, Carrie.'

'Absolutely I can Jim.'

'Tommy told me it was you. He said you visited afterwards to apologise and ask to be forgiven. Guilty conscience. He didn't deserve what you did.'

'Maybe— maybe not. But if you carry on, you know how this will end.'

'Right, that's it!' said Paul as he stepped forward. Without hesitation, James Struck him hard, knocking him to the floor.

Jim turned to me and said, 'This is for poor Tommy, you bitch.' As he raised his hand to strike me.

Paul was just picking himself up from the floor.

As Jim was about to strike me, he paused. Clearly, he felt a strange sensation. I pulled a silly, confused sort of look on my face and pointed to my own nose. At which point James understanding precisely what was meant by my gesture; put his hand to his nose— by now, blood was in full flow.

Now the tear ducts are connected to the throat as are the ears. So, a little Enochian manipulation and we had a scene straight out of a Steven King movie. Blood now flowing from his ears, nose, mouth and most spectacularly, from his eyes. Jim's hands were covered in blood as he tried to stem the bleeding. His eyesight becoming blurred. A panic-stricken look on his face as he looked in total disbelief at the volume of blood.

'Blimey Jim, you need to see a doctor. Blood pressure's a killer.'

'I'll fucking kill you, I swear,' he screamed.

'No, you won't Jim— now fuck off, unless you want to die here today?'

Jim turned and slowly walked off towards the car park. His face, hands and t-shirt covered in blood.

I'd stopped the bleeding by now. A pint or so of blood goes such a long way.

I was initially unaware that Paul, who had seen and heard everything was stood staring at me as if I were some monster.

'What the fuck did you just do to him, Cathy?'

'Nothing— he just had a nosebleed— blood pressure can do that— he was clearly wound up.'

'What like the guy who had the heart attack— and who the fuck is Tommy?'

'Look, let's pack up and go I'm not in the mood anymore.'

'What just like that?— we need to talk Cathy.'

'Then let's talk at home rather than in public, shall we? People are staring at us.'

'Is there any fucking wonder?'

The drive to Pauls apartment was void of any conversation. I had moved into his place some six months earlier.

'Cathy—' started Paul as we threw off our shoes and headed to the lounge.

'What?'

'What the fuck did I just witness?'

'A fucking idiot who had a nosebleed.'

Cathy— I saw you, I heard what you said to him— and what he said to you.'

'We were kids his mate got meningitis and went blind— they all called me a witch and said that I had done it— so it just added fuel to the fire— that's all.'

'Cathy— you talked to me about trust. One of the first things we ever spoke about. I trust you. I trust you to tell me the truth.'

'Yeah— well I don't know that you can be trusted with the truth.'

'Wow— thanks, at least I know where I stand.'

'What is it you want me to say, Paul?'

'Cathy, I know what I saw, and it was unnervingly similar to the incident in the bar the night we met.'

'Okay— I'm a witch. The spawn of hell and the princess of Darkness. How's that?'

'Now you're just being stupid.'

'Really! so you claim that I deliberately gave the guy at the bar a heart attack and just now gave Jim a nosebleed. How the fuck would you explain that exactly?'

'That was not just a nosebleed. It was like watching a fucking horror movie.'

'It was good, wasn't it?'

'No, it wasn't. It was fucking terrifying is what it was.'

'Look— no harm done.'

'Cathy let me ask you again— how did you do that?'

'I'm the spawn of Satan an unholy abomination and generally an evil bitch.'

'The truth— I beg you, Cathy. You're fucking scaring me.'

'You never need to fear me, Paul.'

'Tell me what's going on, Cathy.'

'Okay! If that's what you want.'

'It is—'

I gave Paul the no holds barred version. Laying it all bare. Thomas, Michael, my dad and the two incidents he had witnessed.

There was a long silence as he processed what I had told him. He hadn't asked many questions as I unloaded on him like a Gatling gun.

'Cathy— what the fuck?'

'I guess that's us finished, is it? Shall I pack my things?'

'No, don't be silly— but it's not as if you have just confessed to having an affair or even a drug habit. You're a witch, and you are plagued by this Darkness thing because he wants you to help him destroy mankind— That's if I understand you correctly?'

'In a nutshell— yes.'

'Boy, that's messed up. So, was that the Darkness that I saw today or was it you?'

'Well, I hate to admit. I haven't heard from the Darkness for ages. Maybe even since we met. I hate bullies it brings out a side of me that isn't very pleasant.'

'I'll say— so you were in total control of what you did to both the guy in the bar and to Jim?'

'Absolutely.'

'That's some heartless shit, Cathy.'

'Look that's why I keep a low profile. Once someone triggers me, I have to act. I give them a chance to fuck off out of my face. If they don't, then you've seen the consequences.'

'You get a kick from it, don't you?'

'Oh— maybe a little, yes— I punish those deserving of it— so what if I enjoy it a little—'

'A little too much, I think.'

'Listen. Be glad neither of them was a serious threat— if the Darkness had stepped in, they would both be dead.'

'Dead from freak natural causes.'

'Yeah— it's good, isn't it?'

'No, it isn't fucking good Cathy— for fucks sake.'

'look in two years there have been two minor incidents. It's not like I'm out smiting people on a daily basis. Because I could be.'

'I don't fucking doubt it.'

'I'm not sure that I like your tone, Paul.'

'Well, smite me then.'

'Never— I love you, Paul. I can't imagine that you would ever do something so bad as to deserve a smiting from me.'

'I think I'll have to sleep with one eye open from now on.'

'That won't fucking help you, Paul,' I said in as demonic way as I possibly could and without any help from the Darkness. *It was pretty fucking good.*

'Jesus Christ!'

'He can't fucking help you either,' I said in the same voice.

'Pack it in will you. You're creeping me out.'

'Pussy!'

'Whatever.'

'So, how's it feel to be engaged to the most powerful necromancer to have walked the earth in over five-hundred years— does it give you a hard-on.'

'You are so wrong.'

'Does it?'

'A little. Get your arse over here, you sexy little witch.'

Things, as might be expected, were never quite the same again after our heart to heart. But not in a bad way. Just little things here and there. I guess it isn't every day; you learn that your fiancé is Satan's apprentice.

Chapter 13
Double Betrayal

It was 2006. I was twenty-three, life was good, my powers appeared to be under control — well mostly. I did from time to time inflict minor afflictions of relatively short duration on people who annoyed me beyond an acceptable threshold; the odd bout of diarrhoea for people who I felt were quite simply full of shit. You get the picture. And please don't tell me that given these powers, that you wouldn't do the same.

Paul and I had now been together for five years. His business was booming, and we had set a date to be married the following year.

My sister and I had managed to develop a tolerable relationship, though her deep-seated issues had remained. I was found to be infertile due to a condition where the hypothalamus region of the brain malfunctions causing immature eggs to be released by the ovaries. This was identified when I underwent tests for a severe intolerance to cold. This did not bother me to be honest. The thought that my offspring could inherit my powers was enough for me to put the idea out of my mind completely. Paul and I had discussed this early doors.

Good old Linda though saw this as another opportunity to have one over on me. Quickly getting knocked up by her short-term boyfriend. They married and had a second child. She really thought it bothered me. *Nope!*

Maybe my popularity with the boys affected her, she was better looking — only just but she was. She didn't fuck like me though! Hence the problem. She picked up some of my ex's, when we were younger, but they had hoped she was as good in bed as I was, but maybe a little less demanding as few could keep pace with me — she wasn't even close.

Now we did on occasion have to visit Linda and her family. She took an instant shine to Paul and was always very well behaved when he was around. Paul had commented to me that he couldn't see the problem and didn't understand my hatred of Linda.

I couldn't be bothered; I was happy, and I knew she was flirting with Paul to wind me up. So, I didn't give her the satisfaction.

Linda had decided to call and see Paul at the apartment. I was at work. He was working on his website and blog.

Linda had apparently turned up in tears. This is, according to Paul. Linda has a very different account. But I know Paul was honest at least. Her lies are not worth even paying lip service to.

'Hey— what's wrong, Linda?' asked Paul.
'Martin is leaving me for another woman,' she cried.
'Hey, come on, calm down, let me get you a drink.'
'Thanks, I'll have a gin if you've got one?'
'Err— sure if that's what you want.'
'Oh— I wish I could meet someone like you, Paul. All the boys prefer Cathy, and I don't know why. Everyone says I'm prettier. Do you think I am?'
'You're both gorgeous young women.'
'But am I prettier?'

'Well I guess— there isn't much in it though, and it's not just about looks.'

'So, what then? Is Cathy a better person? More fun than me is that what it is?'

Linda could lay it on thick. She was a clever and manipulative little bitch. She may not be a witch, but she was undoubtedly working her own brand of magic.

'I have no idea Linda, you seem nice, and we have a laugh together on the odd times we meet up. But I don't know you that well to be fair.'

'Perhaps she is just better in bed. Could that be it?'

'Well I can't answer that can I.'

'Look, Paul, I always end up playing second fiddle to Cathy. I need to know what it is that's wrong with me.'

'Look, it's not you. Martins a wanker if he cheated on you.'

'Paul— will you make love to me?'

'What? — NO! — why would you even ask that?'

'I need to know if that's what it is. You can tell me if Cathy is better or not.'

'Linda— stop it.'

'It'll be just a one-off— our secret. I need to know.'

'You need help— but not like this, Linda.'

'Paul— I am attracted to you— if you reject me now, I'll have nothing to live for.'

'What do you mean by that. You have two lovely children.'

'They'd be better off without me.'

'What a ridiculous thing to say.'

'Paul— don't make me beg. Just once, I know you like me, I've seen how you look at me.'

'I do like you, Linda, but I love Cathy.'

'You have no idea what it's been like living in my sister's shadow all these years.'

'So, explain it to me.'

'Cathy was always the favourite.'

'But Cathy told me your dad was disappointed that he didn't get a son. That doesn't sound like she was favourite, and you were closer to your dad than she was.'

'Yeah— but mum just wanted me out of the house so she could spend time with Cathy. Secretly researching witchcraft— I found the books. I knew.'

'But again, that's not Cathy's fault, is it?'

'Do you know she is a witch?'

'I do, yes.'

'So, she told you— funny she never told me— I just guessed.'

'She doesn't have any real power just a bit of mediumship.'

'Don't lie, Paul— you're not very good at it.'

'I still don't understand why you hate her so much for something she can't help.'

'She made me allergic to my own father and then she struck him down and later killed him. Is that not a reason to hate her?'

'That's just silly talk, Linda. Cathy would never do that.'

'You know it's true I can see it in your eyes. Cathy had all the boys swooning over her.'

'Yes— after years of bullying— did you get bullied, Linda?'

'Sticks and stones.'

'She got teased and bullied for years because of how she looked. And you stirred the pot.'

'See everyone takes poor old Cathy's side.'

'I'm trying to be objective, Linda. Do you really hate her that much?'

'She hates me— '

'She hates you because you were a total bitch to her from the day she was born.'

'I just want to be loved, Paul. Nobody loves me.'

'Linda, I don't know what to tell you. Love is a two-way street. You can't just demand that people love you.'

'I love you, Paul.'

'No, you don't.'

'I do. I know you feel it too.'

'Linda, I do like you. You are beautiful, and I do see past the nasty bitch act. But I do not love you.'

'I knew it. Be with me, Paul.'

'I can't Linda. I'm sorry.'

'You're scared of what she will do to you.'

'Yes, I am— but it's not that.'

'Why would you be scared of her? You said she was just a medium.'

'Linda— I think you should go.'

'If I go two things will happen— Firstly I will write a suicide note that says we were lovers and you jilted me. Secondly, I will kill myself.'

'You can't be serious.'

'Look at me— what have I got to lose Paul.'

'Cathy would know it was a last-ditch attempt to spite her.'

'Can you be sure, Paul? Stake your life on it, can you? — cos, you may have to.'

'You are an evil bitch. Thank god you didn't get her powers. We'd all be doomed.'

'So, Paul, fuck me once. I swear on my life that will be it. It'll be enough that I know I fucked her precious fiancé and that she is oblivious to it.'

'If you ever speak of this or try this again. Be assured Cathy will be the least of your worries. You scheming bitch.'

'That's it, Paul— talk dirty. I like that.'

'I mean it, Linda. It's a one-time-only ride.'

'Then you'd better make it a good one. No going through the motions. If I don't feel the love, Paul, then it's no deal. So, you'd better make me cum.'

Linda moved to kiss Paul. He resisted but not for long. Back to the standing prick having no conscience. *Or is that unfair?*

So, arriving home early after a power cut at work. Imagine my surprise at finding Paul with his head between Linda's legs. Catching them fucking like animals would have been better, this was tenderness and intimacy, and it cut me in half.

Time seemed to stand still. I stood there in complete and utter shock at what I saw. The betrayal I felt was beyond words. I had reconciled in my head that there was no level to which my sister wouldn't stoop to get one up on me. But Paul!

I was lost for words. My sister didn't even try and feign shock, guilt or embarrassment.

'Hey, Sis, what are you doing here?' She said with a smirk. Pulling a sheet over her as she spoke.

Seeing the look on my face clearly made her fucking day, if not her year.

'It's my fucking home, that's what I'm doing here,' I replied, 'so what the fuck is this?'

'Hey, babe —' started Paul.

'Shut your mouth!' I interrupted, 'shut your fucking mouth and don't even think about saying it's not what it looks like.'

'Wow, this is awkward,' said Linda smugly.

There was a long, uneasy silence as I continued to process the scene before me. Then the voice, the Darkness— as my wrath began to rise inside me. The voice, my guiding angel — angel of Darkness speaking Enochian the language of angels.

'Strike them down, kill them both!' said my dark angel. 'Do it now.'

I wanted to kill them. I truly did. Paul was dressed now and stood before me.

'She means nothing, it was just a sympathy fuck. I am so sorry, Cathy,' said Paul. He looked remorseful. I looked him in the eyes, revealing nothing but planting my seed of vengeance.

'We are finished,' I replied. Paul knew from my eyes that there was no point trying to reason with me. He walked to the lounge and sat; his head in his hands, sobbing.

'You get dressed and get out you dirty little slut. I will never speak to you again.'

'Oh, Sis. Don't be like that. Is it my fault Paul finds me more attractive than you? He says I'm better in bed too,' she replied; looking to get a further rise from me.

'You can't help it, can you? — Since we were young children, you have resented me for no good reason— always trying to get one up. What did I ever do?' I asked.

'What can I say — I hated you from the start.'

'Well be assured, regardless of what Paul may have said to massage your precious ego — I know for a fact you are not even half as good between the sheets as me. Half-a-dozen of my ex's will attest to that! You hateful little slut. You were always second best and not even a very good one at that.'

Linda was now dressed, she too stood before me, in striking distance of my powers.

'Go now before I do something I will regret,' I said softly. My seed planted.

My sister left with no inkling of what was coming for her and my treacherous fiancé.

I sat on the edge of the bed and sobbed.

Paul came to comfort me.

'Get your filthy cheating hands off me.'

'Look I don't even know what happened Cathy.'

'Ri.... ght— I guess her clothes just fell off by themselves, and as you went to help her, you tripped and landed face down between her legs.'

'Cathy calm down, please.'

'It's too late Paul.'

'Too late for what?'

'To stop me from smiting you.'

'WHAT!'

'You heard me.'

'The fuck have you done?'

'Guess you'll have to wait and see won't you.'

'Reverse it then.'

'I can't.'

'Bitch.'

'Yeah, I warned you from the start. Trust. Without it, there is nothing. You told me if you ever betrayed my trust, you would deserve whatever I did to you.

'Am I going to die?'

'No— that would be too good for you. Now I'm packing my stuff and moving back to mums.'

'Cathy—'

'You have no idea what you have done to me, Paul. I know now that I will never let anyone in again. Ever! — Thanks for that. You have truly broken my heart.'

It seemed as though life would continue to put me in situations where I would act. Where I would use my powers for vengeance. It was from that point that I decided to become reclusive. Shut off from society. I would look to find the cause of my curse, maybe find a cure for it. Until such time though I was a danger, and I knew I had come close to killing both Paul and Linda— seconds away, in fact.

The following day I received a call from Linda's husband telling me that Linda had injured herself lifting something, she had prolapsed a disc in her lower back and looked as though she may now be paralysed from the waist down. Naturally, I already knew this.

A week or so later, Paul called to say he had double testicular torsion, which he informed me was extremely rare and that both his testicles had started to go necrotic and had to be removed.

'Wow, Paul, that's dreadful news,' I said, 'maybe when you were banging Linda you thrust a little too hard — oh well never mind,' I continued, 'Don't call me again you disloyal bastard,' I concluded. I hung up the phone before he could get another word out. He tried for weeks to get me to change my mind. Texting and calling my mums. After a month or so he seemed to get the message.

I felt somehow vindicated, strange as that may sound. Was I self-righteous? As the days went by, I did start and think that I had perhaps been a tad overzealous and disproportionate with my punishments. Did I have the right as I had done with my father? To be judge, juror and executioner? I had ruined their lives— but then they had ruined mine.

Though the punishments fit the crimes in my eyes at least. Did I have the right? Things would never be the same again. Not ever!

Paul should have let Linda kill herself. I would have believed him. I would know. Instead, he fell for her bullshit lies. I told him what she was like. But no. How he ever thought she had an ounce of good in her is beyond me. He fucked my sister! There is no coming back from that. No mitigating circumstances. Sorry, Paul. I thought you were the one. For a time, my life had meaning and purpose outside of my curse. You took that from me. You are no better than the rest. My heart is broken, and the Darkness almost had me. I will never love again. If I were able, I would end my own life right now. Trust no one.

Chapter 14
Going Back to my Roots

I said previously there are rules to using my powers. One such rule is that they simply cannot be used for personal gain. Seems that was not the case for me.

Having decided after paralysing my sister and castrating my boyfriend that I needed to remove myself from society at large. I set about achieving this.

I didn't want to have to work, nor did I want to have to sign-on for benefits. Instead, I hit the casinos and bookies. Systematically over the course of six months, I managed to work my magic. Obviously not wishing to draw attention to myself I was careful. Betting sporadically on various games. Acting the *beginner's luck* routine, and it worked.

I was able to buy a modest property and invest the remainder to provide me with an adequate income.

This freed me up to investigate my heritage, and with modern technology, including DNA comparison, this was made even more accessible.

The answers, however, lead me to believe that my ancestry had been far from accidental.

Indeed, it appeared that somehow, someone or something had worked quite tirelessly to create what was effectively a hybrid witch.

I had links to Jane Fromond, the wife of John Dee, who had by Dee's own accounts, slept with Edward Kelly a gifted scryer. Kelly and John Dee had, according to John Dee's personal diaries — had conversations with angels.

What was strange is that John Dee had a daughter called Katherine, who as it turns out, was also born on the 7th June. I asked my mum if she had named me because of this. She said she had not. Claiming she had never researched John Dee's life, before my interest in the subject.

Dee's diaries attest to the fact, he and Kelly had by the use of the black mirror transcribed the language of angels or Enochian. Enoch, by all accounts, spoke to angels after the death of Adam.

The language of angels unlocks angel magic, the most powerful of all magic — My magic!

It doesn't end there, and it seems that at every opportunity bloodlines were crossed. I had links to witches as far back as the Scottish witch trials.

The powers can skip a generation or even two. It seems I drew the short-straw and received the full complement from all those years of deliberate, selective breeding. Even my dad carried strong genes, though the presence of any gifts in him was absent. It did look as though someone had done some very intelligent matchmaking over the centuries.

I am now fluent in Enochian magic, aided by my reading of John Dee's notes and with help from the voice in my head. The voice that had clearly been behind the manufacture of this super-witch as part of a clandestine breeding programme.

What was also evident was that much as the Darkness wanted to weaponise me. I had to freely give myself over to it. The only other way that it can win my soul is if I were to kill an innocent. Otherwise, the Darkness could not command me.

It is speculated that Edward Kelly had what is known as the philosopher's stone and was able to turn lead and other base metals into gold and silver. During his scrying sessions, Kelly and Dee repeatedly came into contact with an angel or possibly a demon, by the name of Madimi. Dee's daughter, one of eight children, was named Madinia. Accurate accounts of her life are sketchy, to say the least.

I have used the black mirror to scry. It is easy to see how one could be deceived by the entities with which you might converse. Certainly not for the untrained or weak-minded.

So, as a carefully conceived hybrid witch; having been in the making for at least five hundred years. It seems the only powers I do not possess, much to my disappointment and frustration are; teleportation, flight — no not even with a broomstick and telekinesis— Oh, nor can I make myself invisible — *damn it!*

After my run-in with fat boy Thomas. I did consider my role as a pre-emptive punisher. I could set myself up as a medium. Maybe even offer free readings. Once I touch the customer, I can see if they are bad or likely to be bad. Bad in my view, being defined really as a murderer, rapist or other sex offender. If they are destined to do evil, I smite them with some appropriate punishment meaning they will be unable to carry out those crimes.

However, the guilt I felt over my dad and Thomas, then further compounded by what I did to Linda and Paul had left me jaded. I decided against it. I had no right. Regardless of how I tried to justify it.

Instead, I became an almost celibate hermit. I say almost. I do get booty-called by a couple of my ex's from time to time.

I did still have a deep longing to use my gift for good. This meant using my various *clairs* to help people where I could. While at the same time trying to keep low-key. This was a conundrum alright. It would, though, in the end, solve itself.

Chapter 15
Using my Clairs

So, I'm sure you have all heard of a clairvoyant? Someone with the ability to see objects, actions, or events distant from the present and without the use of eyes. Clairvoyance transcends time and space. But there are many more; such as Claircognizance which is an explicit knowledge without any physical explanation or reason. Claircognizance includes precognition and retrocognition.

There are others that cover smell, intuitive knowing by touching. I do possess the full set.

I am thankfully able to switch this on and off; otherwise, I would be bombarded by spirits with messages. Trust me, it sounds great, but it never stops. I sympathise with those mediums unable to switch off from this constant white noise.

Anyway, there I am it's 2008 some two years on from my split with Paul. I'm sat reading the local rag. The main story is the murder of a local man. A young father, slane in front of his wife and young son. The story is heartbreaking; written by Stephanie Turner. The article was written with passion and empathy. It seems the poor man who was named Graham, had no criminal ties. Yet he appeared to have been deliberately targeted. The killer shouting him by his name before shooting him dead and riding off on his motorcycle along with an accomplice.

The Police claimed to have no leads whatsoever.

As I began to let, my thoughts drift. I looked at the photograph of this young man, pictured with his wife and son. I suddenly connected.

The conversation was bitty and fragmented, but as an experienced practitioner, I was able to piece together what was being presented to me. In summary, what I gleaned over the course of an hour— In plain English was as follows:

'Is this the spirit of Graham?'

'Yes, I am Graham.'

'Do you have a message for someone Graham?'

The voice I was hearing was soft, a little unsure, a little scared.

'What is going on?' he asked.

It is hard when the death has been sudden and recent. The spirit often is unaware it has passed.

'Graham — you were shot — do you remember?' I asked cautiously.

'I remember — and I know why.' He started to sound angry.

'Graham, what happened was dreadful, I can help you put it right if you let me.'

For a moment I thought he had gone.

'How?' he asked.

'Do you know who killed you?'

'No not the man who shot me, but the man who paid him to.'

'Okay — So who?'

'My boss Edward Stead.'

'Why would your boss have you killed?'

'Look, it's complicated. The company sells and hires out heavy plant and machinery. They have recently started importing equipment from Mexico.'

'So, what's the issue with that.'

'The issue is — the machinery is loaded with cocaine. It is manufactured into the steel box section, so you need to destroy the machine to get to it. Customs would never think to check inside welded box section that is integral to the machinery, it's not like its stuffed into the tyres or behind the dashboard.'

'How did you find out?' and how did they know you'd found out?'

'Well, I am a technician, and I needed a hydraulic pump for an on-site repair, and we had none in stock. So, I knew we had just taken delivery of a new machine that would be at least a week having all its pre-delivery inspections and so on. I ordered a new pump but went to the new machine to take its pump temporarily until the new pump arrived.'

'Okay, I guess you didn't ask permission?'

'No, I was just trying to get the customer up and running.'

'And?'

'Well I went into the main garage where new stock is stored, it is like an old aircraft hangar.'

'You were seen?'

'No, not directly, I went to the new machine and noticed it had been cut up. Specifically, the main box section of the hydraulic platform. Packs of drugs were laid out.'

'Did you take the pump you had gone in for?'

'No, I legged it.'

'Someone saw you?'

'I was seen on a hidden camera.'

'Okay, so I need to contact the police.'

'No — the police are involved, I saw someone I recognised in the boss's office, they looked good friends. I knew the officer from a previous encounter when I was giving a statement about a violent mugging that I had witnessed.'

'Okay then so what should I do?'

'Why don't you contact the journalist?'

I pondered for a moment.

'Okay, leave that with me, do you have a message for your wife and son?'

'Not yet — Once this is over, I will.'

'I will reach out to you, Graham.'

With that, the connection was lost.

This was precisely the type of thing I had been looking for, helping but at the same time maintaining a low profile. The journalist can take all the credit, my name entirely out of the picture.

'Hello, can I speak to Stephanie Turner please?' I asked as the woman answered the telephone at the West London Gazette.

'May I ask what it is regarding?'

'Yes, it's about the murder of Graham Wainwright,' I replied.

'Stephanie Speaking — how might I help?'

'I have information regarding your story.'

'What information is that?' Stephanie asked me, her curiosity piqued.

'I don't want to talk on the phone,' I replied. *I'd always wanted to say that!* This was going to be cloak and dagger. I was quite excited.

'Well, where shall we meet then?'

'You need to come to my home, but you must not tell anyone,' I said, to further build some tension and atmosphere.

'When would be convenient and where exactly are you,' she asked.

'I'm only ten minutes from your office, early tomorrow would be good for me,' I suggested gleefully.

'Okay — sorry, what's your name?'

'It's Catherine Heely, my address is 178 Station Road.'

'Okay, Catherine, shall we say 9:00 a.m.?'

'That's fine, you can call me Cathy.'

'Fine Cathy — I'm Steph. See you in the morning.'

Next morning, I sprang out of bed, showered and made a coffee and a slice of toast. I Waited patiently and with a degree of excitement and anticipation for my guest.

A ring of the bell at 8:55a.m. signalled the prompt arrival of Steph. I do hate people with poor timekeeping. *This was a good start.*

'Hi, I'm Steph. You must be Cathy?'

'Yes — do come in Steph. Can I get you a drink?'

'Coffee would be good thanks, white, one sugar please.'

Manners— another plus.

'So, Cathy, what can you tell me about the murder of poor Graham?' asked Steph as I handed her the coffee.

'Steph, first of all, I need to explain to you a couple of things. Please do not think me crazy I can assure you I am not.'

Steph quite rightly paused and looked as though she had made the short journey to speak to some crackpot.

'Okay,' she said hesitantly, 'what is it I need to know?'

'Well, in simple terms, I am a very gifted medium.'

I could see immediately that she was firmly in the non-believer camp. Deciding whether or not it would be rude to leave without finishing her coffee.

'Please, at least drink your coffee,' I said, 'If you want to leave after that, you can.'

Steph looked at me, wondering if I had read the look on her face or her mind. *A little of both.*

'You're a sceptic, aren't you Steph?'

'I have never given it much thought, to be honest,' she replied.

'So, if I told you I have a young man named Ademar with me, he wants to say *Te Quiero.*'

Steph looked at me in disbelief, her eyes instantly filling with tears.

'Is this some sort of sick joke?'

'Why would I joke about that Steph? I can describe him if you'd like?'

Steph was now openly sobbing. She looked at me, still unsure if I was the real deal.

'He says he is with you always and not to blame yourself for what happened,' I continued.

'You are for real?'

'Yes — I am for real and I have been contacted by Graham, he knows who killed him and why. He says the police or at least one senior officer is also involved.'

'So, what is it all about?'

'Drugs,' I replied.

'I might have known; I thought the police didn't seem that interested.'

I filled Steph in on what Graham had told me. She was fired up alright.'

'Ademar, says to be careful, you are going to be treading on some familiar toes.'

Steph stopped and looked at me — she was clearly affected deeply by the messages I had relayed to her.

'This will need some serious thought and planning,' started Steph, 'let me ponder on this for a few days, I will do some digging around. If I need more specifics, can you help?'

'Of course I can, do be careful Steph.'

'I need to leave, I feel a little overwhelmed, but I want to see you again, Cathy, for a more relaxed chat. If that's okay?'

'It is — I can sense you are a good woman Steph. All I ask is that you keep our relationship strictly between us. I am your confidential informant.'

'Absolutely Cathy — thank you so much,' replied Steph, as she continued tearily, 'I'm in total shock.'

'It's perfectly normal — take care and see you soon.'

We swapped telephone numbers, and I walked her to the door — we hugged like old acquaintances, and she left, wiping tears from her eyes, while at the same time attempting to fully regain her composure.

Chapter 16
Heart to Heart

A single long buzz from the doorbell signalled Steph's arrival, two weeks on from our initial meeting.

'Come on in,' I said as I opened the door to greet her. She was holding a bunch of flowers. We hugged; kissing each other on the cheek. We did seem like old friends. I had felt a powerful bond to Steph from the outset.

'Coffee white one?' I offered. Taking the flowers from her. 'They are lovely. Thank you.'

'Perfect,' replied Steph as she seated herself in the lounge.

'Much to report? I shouted from the kitchen.

'Plenty,' she replied enthusiastically.

I Handed her the coffee and placed a vase containing the flowers she had bought me in the middle of the coffee table.

'Do tell,' I said eagerly.

'I've been digging around and the plant machinery sales and hire business is wholly owned by a larger corporation not registered in the UK. The true ownership is proving very difficult to determine.'

'So, it is a front or more specifically a very clever drug import business.'

'It would seem so; I have a contact in serious crimes at the Met. I have spoken to him about the situation, they have now opened a case and will start building a better understanding and try to identify the senior officer that Graham had mentioned.'

'Well I can just ask Graham if he remembers the name of the officer, it might speed things along.'

'What— just like that?'

'Sure. Get your notebook ready.'

I opened the channels and within a minute or so I had reached Graham. He was a little easier to communicate with. But still not wholly clear.

'Graham, do you remember the name of the police officer you saw with your boss?'

'DCI Salter was his name.'

'DCI Salter,' I spoke out for Steph's benefit. She quickly scribbled the name in her notebook.

'Is there anything else you know that could help us, Graham?'

'No! I wish I could do more; I have tried to spy on them, but while I can see them, I am unable to hear what they are saying. Why is that?'

'Graham, in time you may develop the ability, but some spirits never do, It's complicated and obviously frustrating for you. We are on the case,' I replied as we severed the connection.

Steph was looking intently at me.

'Well?' she asked.

'That's it for now.'

'Well, it's something at least. I will get this to my contact.'

'So, what's your story?' I asked.

'Where should I start?'

'How about Ademar?' I suggested.

Steph nodded, I think she half expected me to say that, as her eyes again became teary.

'In a nutshell, Ademar was a lovely young man. I was investigating drug cartels in Bolivia and was living with his family. I gained his trust. He, as did about one in eight Bolivians at the time, earned his living from the drug trade. I got found out. I knew he was a little smitten with me, and I used him. He was in love with me. Enforcers turned up at the house. He died in place of me. His last words were that he loved me. Or *Te Quiero* in Spanish.'

'That's awful Steph. It wasn't your fault, though, and Ademar doesn't blame you.'

'It was my fault! I should have been more careful. Is he here now?' she asked.

'Yes, he is — he wants you to find love Steph, the kind of love he had for you.'

With that Steph began to cry openly, I moved over to comfort her as she wept. After several minutes she blew her nose, wiped her eyes and said, 'I will never find a love like that.'

'Steph, I can tell you that you will, I can see you finding love, it's a way off, but you will fall in love.'

'Really! I'll fuck it up like I always do.'

'It's a little too far in the future for me to see detail, just have faith. Faith is the key.'

'That's enough about me for today. What's your story?'

'You won't believe my story. You're a sceptic remember.'

'I think it's safe to say I'm a convert. You are amazing.'

'Steph, I trust you. I Don't trust anyone anymore, so that is a huge statement.'

'Well I'm honoured, I will never betray that.'

'I know— I am going to tell you everything, maybe not all in one go but no one except my mum and my ex knows the truth.'

'What truth?'

'That I am a powerful necromancer, that I have powers beyond your comprehension and understanding.'

'What? You mean beyond talking to spirits?'

'That is the tame end of my powers.'

'So, what can you do?'

'I have the ability to influence the natural world.'

'Meaning what exactly?'

I picked out one of the roses from the vase. I held it in my hand. Steph looked on, intrigued. The rose withered in my hand; the petals fell to the floor.

'Oh my god!' exclaimed Steph, with a look of horror mixed with amazement at what she witnessed.

'I can effectively do the same to people and animals!'

'What?'

'I could kill you by simply looking in your eyes.'

Steph looked at me in horror.

'Do you still want to be friends?' I asked.

'Yes— I think so.'

'Then, I will continue.'

'How can you do that? How is that even possible? Have you ever killed anyone?'

'Okay— it seems I am the product of deliberate breeding; manipulated over hundreds of years. The intention to produce a super-witch and I'm it— Yes I killed a boy who was trying to rape me and would likely have killed me— and I killed my own father!'

My own eyes now filled with tears. I was laying it all bare to someone who I barely knew. But who I felt so inexplicably attached to.'

'You killed your dad? Why would you do that?'

'It was in a moment of fear and anger. My dad attacked my mum and then was going to beat me too! I struck him down by giving him a stroke but didn't kill him at first, it was only after months of watching him suffer that I finished the job.'

'Oh, Cathy— I'm so sorry.'

'I have a voice in my head, I call it the Darkness. It wants me to embrace evil and do its bidding, but I won't succumb to it. Which is why I chose this life of solitude.'

'A voice in your head?' replied Steph in a manner clearly suggesting that I have a psychological affliction.

'I have considered that I may suffer from Schizophrenia and Psychosis having investigated these conditions I do I admit exhibit many of the symptoms.'

'Have you seen anyone on a professional basis?'

'No because I know its real, and yes being in a delusional state is a symptom, but it does not explain my abilities does it? Maybe science is wrong, maybe if you look at the symptoms then a less palatable truth is demonic possession; if not possession then demonic interference. Just because science can't prove or disprove this, does not mean that it is not so.'

'Maybe you have a point Cathy. I can't believe it; This is just beyond my comprehension. Witches are real?'

'Is it so hard to believe? Two weeks ago, you didn't believe in mediumship.'

'My mind is blown. Seriously, I consider myself to be rational, grounded and openminded. This is something else. It must be hard for you, Cathy. I can see the pain in your eyes.'

'It is tough— and I have come close to giving in to it. Power is seductive, there is no doubt. The things I could do if I embraced the Darkness would be apocalyptic. That's not exaggerating. Trust me on that.'

'I believe you, Cathy— let's be glad you are a good person.'

'That's part of the problem Steph— I'm not— I know I am bad. Deep down, I am evil. I strike out in vengeful wrath. I hurt and kill people as a result. All I do is suppress the Darkness and try against the odds to be good. I'm ultimately fighting against who I really am.'

'No! — You are good at heart; you are fighting against this Darkness. It is the Darkness trying to turn you.'

'You are kind Steph. You are also a little naive but in a nice way.'

'Yeah — I get called that quite a lot.'

'It is said that people are considered naïve because they try and see the good in people. I guess it's a sad indictment of society.'

'Thank you— that's what I tell people.'

'Do you want another coffee?'

'I think I need something stronger.'

'I can get you something?'

'Better not— I'm driving.'

'Stay over, we can get takeout and have a few drinks. Make it a girly night in,' I offered.

Steph paused for a moment. I could sense her thoughts.

'I won't cast a spell on you or try to seduce you— well not unless you want me to.'
'Okay— let's do it.'
'How does Pizza sound?'
'Good to me.'
'I bet you're a red wine girl? Am I right?'
'You are. — Mind-reading me again, are you?'
'I Don't know what you mean— I have Merlot, Rioja or Malbec?'
'Malbec please.'
'Good choice.'

We agreed on toppings and ordered the food. Once delivered, we settled into easy conversation. Comparing stories of conquests, lost virginity and best lovers. As it approached the witching hour and three bottles of Malbec in. We were both a little giddy.

'Have you ever slept with a woman Steph?' I asked.
'When I was at Uni— I did once.'
'Did you not like it then.'
'It was okay— I prefer men, even though they can be total dicks at times.'
'Hey— so can women.'

The bond I felt with Steph was strong. I knew she felt it too. Not in a sexual way, though there was very clearly a degree of sexual tension between us. I knew she was mulling over the possibility we might share a bed.

'I better make up the spare bed before I'm too pissed to do it,' I said, breaking the momentary silence, 'unless you're cool jumping in with me. No strings, I promise.'

'I can't promise the same,' said Steph. Herself surprised that those words had slipped from her lips.

'I think you're a little bit tipsy there Steph.'
'A little— but I know what I'm saying.'
'Okay— I really would like to show you a good time Steph. Let's be clear on what this is though.'
'I know what it is Cathy. It is a one time, never to be repeated experience.'
'I agree— this will cement us as friends for life. We will connect at a spiritual level Steph, and you will never be quite the same again— but in a nice way.'
'Are you really that good.'
'Well, yes I am, but I'm not talking about just the physical aspect— there will be a spiritual transference I can feel it now. We were destined to meet you and me— this is not the beginning of a love story. What we have will transcend that. I cannot promise that it will necessarily be a happy ending either— the Darkness might win the day.'
'I will take that chance Cathy I feel the connection too.'
'Let's go to bed then.'
The night was torrid and tender it felt so natural. I felt closer to Steph than I had any other living soul. It was inexplicable— but it was! Nonetheless.
I was making coffee when Steph appeared in the kitchen and sat at the dining table.
'Morning,' she said.
'Good morning— how are you this morning?'
'I can't explain how I feel Cathy— enriched somehow.'
'Good— that was some night.'
'It was— not sure I could do that on a regular basis.'
'But you're good— yes?'
'I am— strange— this morning after thing— doesn't seem remotely awkward.'

'Well, that's because we know it is what it is. A one-off! We have no expectations; we have cemented what is much more than a simple friendship. We will not complicate that friendship by becoming involved sexually, so what could be easier? — want some toast?'

'Sure, a couple of slices if that's okay?'

'No problem, here's your coffee.'

'Cheers.'

With that, the whole night before was forgotten, well not forgotten, but you get the picture. The conversation returned to the Graham situation, and Steph eventually left at around 10:30a.m.

Chapter 17
Out of the Frying Pan and Into the Scryer

As part of my research into my ancestry, my potential connection to the Dee's and Kelly's intrigued me. John Dee was one of the greatest minds of his time and adviser to Queen Elizabeth I.

It is speculated that he used angel magic to cause the Spanish Armada to flounder in the stormy seas.

John Dee and Edward Kelly over many years documented their endeavours using a Black Mirror to scry. Edward Kelly was the Scryer. Their detailed diaries are often referred to as the conversations with angels.

These conversations resulted in the transcribing of the language of angels or the Enochian language. This was the original language spoken before the fall of man and his expulsion from the garden of Eden.

Understanding the language of Angels is said to unlock Angel Magic the most powerful of all magic.

I managed to source myself a black mirror which was made under the light of a full moon.

Though it is also possible to use the screen of a modern tv or smartphone as a black mirror if you know what you are doing.

Now the idea is that focusing on a black mirror detaches you from our reality; some say it opens the door to another plane.

I had not scryed for many years, but I decided to give it another go after recent events with Steph and Graham.

I Reached it down from my mantlepiece, I placed it carefully on my dining table. A single candle placed behind the mirror. Curtains closed and the light's off.

As I cleared my mind, I heard a voice.

'A ors trian quansb g.'

This was Enochian!

'What do you mean the Darkness will destroy me?'

'g trian adoian telco lrasd tia ozien.'

'I will face death at his hands? Who is this?

'Ol zir Madimi.'

'Madimi? — I know that name. You are the angel Madimi. One of the Angels that spoke with Dee and Kelly?'

'Yes, I am she— your grasp of Enochian is good, you have the power of angel magic.'

'I have a constant voice in my head. The Darkness speaks to me in Enochian. I had no choice but to learn it. When I say learn it— I just seemed to know it, if that makes sense.'

'You have great power, Catherine. He wants you by his side. He will not rest until you succumb to him.'

'I know, but he can't have me unless I agree to it or unless I kill an innocent, locking myself away puts me out of reach.'

'ge vaoan.'

'What do you mean not true.'

'He can be persuasive. You will need all of your strength when the time comes Catherine.'

'Well, I can be equally as stubborn.'

'You sense it, Catherine. Why else would you have prepared Stephanie?'

'It's not like that Madimi.'

'noib t l od g om t.'
'No, I don't know it! It isn't like that.'
'She doesn't know what you did to her, does she?'
'I told you— it's not like that.'
'I can sense your fear, Catherine.'
'Obviously, I am terrified of meeting the Darkness. I know he will come for me! I am frightened to death that I will give in to his demands.'
'Stay strong. Stay focussed.'
'Easy for you to say.'
'g balit capimao tia trian niis.'
'*In good time he will come*. Well thanks, Madimi your words of Enochian wisdom are so encouraging. Are you able to show yourself Madimi? Dee, I think, was in love with you. So much so he named a daughter after you.'
'Yes — '

I sensed movement to my left. Turning to look there stood a beautiful woman with flowing red hair, wearing a green satin gown. She had a full and voluptuous figure. I suppose to describe her as angelic is too simplistic, but in the truest sense, that is what she was. I remembered some of the Dee diaries.

'Did Dee not question your mother, Galvah. Saying that Trithemius had said; that no good angel ever appeared in the female form?'

'Yes, and I say to you the same as my mother said to Dee. Wisdom is always painted with a woman's garment; for than the pureness of a virgin, nothing is more commendable.'

'You are breathtaking Madimi— truly you are.'

Madimi smiled, I knew that demons could disguise themselves as angels, and some had suggested that Madimi had been demonic. I got no sense of anything other than pure love.

'I must go now,' said Madimi, 'we will commune again soon.'

I poured myself a large glass of wine and retired to my lounge to ponder my angelic conversation.

Chapter 18
Testing Times

It was a couple of weeks after my conversation with Madimi. Steph had arrived and was sat eagerly waiting to update me on the murder case.

'So, any developments?' I asked.

It was as though she had been awaiting the go-ahead as she rattled off the update.

'Well DCI Salter has been on the radar before, he is suspected of corruption, but he is smart. At least now they have some degree of focus. I have applied for a job at Graham's old company they had advertised for an administration manager; I am more than qualified, and I have an interview next week.'

'Is that not a little bit risky Steph?'

'I'll be fine. Seriously. I reckon if I flash a bit of leg and a bit of tit, he'll be putty in my hands.'

'I'm sure. Don't forget your best smoulderingly sultry look.'

'Always,' she replied, giving me precisely that very look.

'Yup, that's the one,' I laughed.

'I only need a week or two to get some concrete information that my contact can act on.'

'Remember what they did to Graham for far less.'

'I know. I'm a big girl.'

'Steph, these people do not just play rough. They kill people. I have many powers, but I cannot make you bulletproof.'

'It won't come to that I promise. Anyway, you said I was going to fall in love in the distant future, so I must be safe.'

'It doesn't work like that Steph. Your Journey can end tomorrow at the hand of someone exercising their own free will.'

'Oh!'

'Yes, Oh, indeed. So be careful.'

We chatted for another hour or so. General chit chat. We had a similar sense of humour and bounced off one another. Steph always lifted my spirit. I was sure if needs be, I would lay down my life for her. Was I though, through my attachment to her? Putting her in danger. The Darkness was devious.

'So, Steph, I'm twenty-five, you're what twenty-seven?'

'Twenty-eight.'

'We could have a bright future as a crime-solving duo.'

'What like Cagney and Lacey?' Joked Steph.

'Laurel and bloody Hardy more like,' I laughed.

'Yeah, we could do so much good. It really is quite exciting.'

'I have wanted to use my gift for good for so long. I now feel I have an outlet. I don't want to waste this gift— but nor do I want to use it for evil. It's tough walking the very thin line.'

'I know. But we can make this work, Cathy.'

Chapter 19
A Mothers Love

My mother had continued to live in the family home. She had many happy memories there, and my father had life insurance in place. The policy paid off the house and left a hefty sum. So, mother dear was quite comfortable. She continued her job at the library.

I never visited her. I left the house only when I absolutely needed to; Such was my concern for what I might do.

Mother did, however, visit me; most weeks, usually on a Sunday. To be fair, she never tried to force me back into contact with Linda. That ship had well and truly sailed after I caught her in bed with Paul.

Mum was aware of how Linda had ended up in a wheelchair and why Paul now had no balls.

Mum was just glad I had not killed her other daughter; and that I had resisted the Darkness.

This Sunday was no different. She arrived just after lunch.

As we got settled with a coffee. Mother looked at me with trepidation.

'Cathy— I have a message for you,' she started hesitantly.

'From who?'

'From the Darkness.'

'What sort of message?' I asked, 'and why can't he tell me directly?'

'Well for a start Cathy, you have warded your home against him, unless he was invited over the threshold, he cannot enter, nor can he hear your thoughts or speak to you as he once could.'

'Well, that was the general idea, mum.'

'Yes, I know. He is becoming impatient.'

'Yeah, well tough shit.'

'Cathy, he wants you to willingly give yourself to him. Completely.'

'It is never going to happen, mum.'

'I know, and I'm glad you feel that way— I truly am.'

'I sense a but!'

'Not a but, just a consequence.'

'And what is that— pray tell?'

'That I die.'

'WHAT!'

'If you don't choose him, he will have me horribly murdered.'

Mum was now in tears, as was I.

'I'm here to tell you, stay strong Cathy. This is his last play. He knows I am all you care about.'

I had considered many potential plays the Darkness might make. Killing or threatening my loved ones was a scenario I had pondered many times. Not only would I become eternally damned, but I would kill countless people. Maybe even bring about the apocalypse.

This, however, had always been speculative. It was now a reality.

'All my affairs are in order Cathy. My will leaves everything to you and your sister. You already have all my books.'

'Mum I don't want or need any of it. I can't bear the thought of what he might do to you.'

'Cathy he can't hear us here. I will take my own life tonight. I have prepared everything. He knows there is no point going after Linda as you wouldn't care if she died.'

'That's unfair mum. She is my sister.'

'Who are you trying to kid Cathy? Linda has always been a horrible, spiteful little girl. I love her because as her mother, I must.'

'So, what are you going to do? Although I'm not sure, I want to know— '

'I will have a hot bath, A glass of wine and your dad's old cut-throat razor.'

'I cannot believe this is happening— how are we discussing your suicide? I will give him what he wants. He will doubtless get me in the end anyway.'

'He won't Cathy. You are strong. You are good. He is desperate. You have outwitted him.'

'So, live with me. The house is warded, he can't get us here.'

'We can't remain in the confines of these four walls forever, Cathy. He will find a way. He will send someone for me. A mortal. A foot soldier.'

Mum was right. The Darkness could not himself enter my home without an invite. But he had many foot soldiers who could. Mere mortals who owed him a favour.

'Then let me take you. Die here. Die in my arms. It will be quick and painless I promise you, mum. I can't bear you going back home alone.'

'Are you sure you can do it, Cathy. It is easy to say. Less easy to do.'

'I ended dad's life to save him from suffering. If the Darkness gets to you first, he will make you suffer to the end. He will make it long and painful.'

'Cathy— I would like that very much— I had hoped you would offer. But I was not going to ask it of you.'

'Wait, though— will I not be killing an innocent, will I not be damned. Will, he not have won?'

'This is a mercy killing, I ask it off you, and I forgive you, just as your father did! Your slate will remain clean.'

'Oh, mum— come here.'

We hugged for what seemed like forever. Sobbing uncontrollably as we did.

As we seemed all cried out. My mum pushed back and looked at me.

'I'm sorry that in bringing you into this world, I also cursed you.'

'Oh, mum no, it's not your fault. I have done some good things with the *gift* you gave me. I will continue to do good until the day I die. So, don't you dare be sorry for that? I felt your love for me always. From the womb to right here and now. I have always loved you. I never have and never will blame you for what I carry with me.'

'I had you when I was twenty-five— You are now twenty-five. You have navigated some very stormy waters, Cathy. But you made it through. I just hate that your journey is far from over and that stormier waters lay ahead.'

'But I have all that you have taught me. I have your wisdom, and I will fight the Darkness to my last breath.'

'I am so very proud of you, Cathy. You will never know just how much I love you.'

'But I do mum.'

'Thank you, Cathy. I will wait for you on the other side.'

'I looked her in the eyes. We shared that final moment as I held her close. She nodded to me as my eyes streamed with tears. I slowed her heart gradually; listening to its beat become softer and softer until it was no more. I felt her spirit leave her body. It hovered for a moment. Before the kitchen lightbulb popped. *Her final goodbye*. With that, she was gone.

I sat holding her for an hour before calling the ambulance. I wanted to lash out at the Darkness. I wanted to step outside free from my warded house. I wanted to summon him. I wanted to fight him. To kill him. But I knew it was futile. To summon him would play into his hands. He knew that. That was his plan B. in fact that was probably his plan A. he knew my temper, my anger; was my Achilles heel.

The worst of it; I could not attend the funeral. I told Linda I wanted nothing from the estate. She could have it all. She would have contested the will anyway. I couldn't give her the satisfaction of dishonouring mums final wishes.

I hoped and prayed that the Darkness was not aware of my relationship with Steph. Her I cared about. I knew I would still let her die before I would give myself to him. Hopefully, he knew that too.

Chapter 20
Sleeping With The Enemy

Not long after my mum had died. In fact, the week after her funeral. I received an unexpected visitor.

It was Thursday, mid-morning. My doorbell buzzed. I rarely had visitors. The odd Amazon delivery and my takeout's. But these were always expected.

This, however, was not. Sure, I did get the odd cold caller, but I had a sign on my door saying if you have not made an appointment then basically take a hike.

I opened the door. Security chain engaged and I peered through the gap.

'Hello, Cathy— DCI Lyons. Do you remember me?' he asked as he flashed his ID at me.

I closed the door to remove the chain and asked him in.

'To what do I owe this unexpected pleasure Officer?' I asked.

'Look you are no longer a child call me Brian,' he replied.

'So— Brian, what can I do for you?'

'Well, can you spare me say an hour. If it's not convenient, I can arrange to call back at a more suitable time.'

'You can have as long as you like Brian. I don't get many visitors. Can I get you a tea or coffee?'

'If that's no trouble. Coffee black, strong and no sugar, please.'

It had been some ten years since our last encounter. Maybe he was part of the investigation into the death of poor Graham. But surely Steph would have given me a heads-up.

'There you go— help yourself to a biscuit, If I'd known you were coming, I would have bought doughnuts in,' I said, with a grin.

'I see you haven't lost your sarcastic streak, Cathy,' he replied, grinning as he chomped a gingernut.

We both chuckled.

'So, Brian. What brings you to my door after all these years?'

Brian was a good ten years older than me. He was stocky but not fat. His hair was shaved close, he had a goatee. Not bad looking actually.

He paused a good while. Looking intently at me and trying to figure out how best to start the conversation.

'Well you need to bear with me,' he started.

'Go on.'

'I understand your mother died recently— I'm sorry.'

'Thank you. But that's not why you are here is it Brian— don't be coy now?'

'Well, in part, it is. Her death certificate said she had died of Commotio Cordis.'

'Or in simple terms a heart attack.'

'Well it is, but not a normal one. You see, Commotio Cordis is usually the result of trauma to the chest wall. As a result, the electrical signals that control the heart cease, and the heart stops. But your mother had no signs of any trauma to her breastbone.'

'I don't understand what you are inferring Brian.'

'Well, it is extremely unusual, you see a normal heart attack leaves a scar on the heart. With Commotio Cordis.

There is no scar. But how did the electrical signal get interrupted? It is very odd.'

'Look, my mum died in my arms. It seemed very sudden, but much as I would have expected a heart attack to be like.'

'Yes, I am aware she died here.'

'Sorry I am not sure what it is you are trying to imply Brian.'

'Well let me finish, maybe it will make more sense once I'm done.'

'Well, I hope so. Can I ask what your interest is in my mother's death?'

'We received a tip-off about your mum's death—effectively saying all may not be as it appears.'

From my sister, I bet.

'It's clearly malicious! Was it a woman?'

'It was a woman, yes. But it was anonymous.'

She just can't help herself—

'So what's your interest?'

'My interest is in you, Cathy, not your mother.'

'In Me?'

'Yes! — You see I visited your sister earlier in the week— Monday I think it was. She doesn't seem to think much of you. I got the impression that you're not that close.'

'No, we never really hit it off. She will have told you that my mother's entire and rather substantial estate was transferred to her at my request; before you accuse me of topping my mother for the money.'

'Yes, she told me that. And I don't for one moment think that.'

'So, what then?'

'Well, she told me her tales of woe. All about her getting caught in bed with your fiancé and how she and he were struck down horribly within days.'

'Yeah, a dose of instant karma if you ask me.'

'She also told me about your dad. How he was arguing with your mum. How she ran to her bedroom in tears. The next thing your fit, strong and healthy father had a massive stroke.'

'These things happen. It was dreadful to see.'

'I'm sure it was Cathy—The thing is I asked her if anyone else she knew, or perhaps that you knew had been mysteriously struck down. What do you think she told me?'

'I have no idea, Brian.'

'Do you remember Thomas Crossland?'

'The name rings a bell— Oh, yes, he used to pick on me at school.'

'And then he contracted meningitis.'

'Oh, that's right he did. Dreadful to be struck down at such a young age.'

'Yes— it was you who found him collapsed, wasn't it?'

'My you have been a busy little bee, haven't you, Brian?'

'I paid Thomas a visit too— I asked him what had happened; as you were the one who found him collapsed.'

'And?'

'Well, he looked terrified if I'm honest. He wouldn't say anything at all.'

'What did you expect him to say?'

'You tell me, Cathy.'

'And how would I know?'

'Cathy. Do you not feel it strange that people who cross you end up with serious afflictions or like your dad and Michael end up dead?'

'Seven years ago, you were in a bar with your fiancé. There was some sort of altercation, and a man had a heart attack.'

'That's right; he wound himself up to the point his heart stopped.'

'Well, that's what the witnesses said. Someone called it in before he collapsed as they feared a fight was about to start. There was nothing to investigate based on the statements we took. But the bar had security cameras.'

'Well then proof absolute that I never laid a finger on him.'

'That's true— but look at this,' Said Brian, as he clicked on a video clip on his phone and passed it over to me.

'What am I looking at Brian?'

'Look at your eyes— just before he collapses, they seem to almost glow.'

'It's the lighting; it was all mood lighting in there if I recall, I think the technical term is flaring Brian; that's what Paul used to call it, that's the thing with digital cameras it's all to do with the CMOS image sensor or something I think— not that I'm trying to tell you your job.'

'No— cos you'd never dream of doing that would you? So, you're sticking with that are you?'

'Well— I can see how it might look. But are you suggesting that it is somehow all down to me?'

'Cut the crap, Cathy. I know what you did at the end of your interview with me. You couldn't help but give me a glimpse. You were just a little bit too cocky. A fuck you.

From you to me. And thanks for the dose of diarrhoea that you left me with.'

'So, what are you saying? are we back to witchcraft, are we? — do you know how ridiculous that sounds?'

'Cathy— since that day, I have become obsessed with the whole subject. Maybe I wanted to wipe that smug grin off of your face, but it fascinates me. You are a witch I know it. I just want to know what that's like? How you manage it all. I can't even imagine what it must be like having the powers that you have.'

'I guess you got me bang to rights, Brian. What are you going to charge me with?'

'I know— I can't— to be honest, I don't think it was all down to you. I maybe saw a frightened little girl with powers that she didn't have full control of. But why your mum? What did she do?'

So here I am. Good old Brian seems to have pieced it all together. *My own fault! I guess I was being cocky*. Is he friend or is he foe though?

'What is it that you want Brian?'

'I want you to be honest. I know Michael was self-defence, certainly the first time. I think you toyed with him in your kitchen. I think you could have let him live had you wanted to. But I perhaps understand why you didn't. I don't get why you killed your mum though.'

'How strongly do you believe in your theory, Brian?'

'I am one hundred per cent sure you are a witch and a powerful one at that.'

'Do you believe I am evil, Brian?'

'That I don't know.'

'Then you have taken a huge risk coming here alone. You look like a stage four pancreatic cancer sufferer,' I teased.

Brian looked at me. Trying to read me. *Was he in danger?*

'Can you be trusted, Brian. Do you want to expose me? Burn me at the stake?'

'I just need to know Cathy. It has consumed me since you showed me what lurks within you.'

'What— you'd like a demonstration, would you?'

'It is so far-fetched. I can't believe I seriously believe it. But I do.'

'Have you spoken to anyone else about your concerns?'

'What so that they can laugh at me?'

'Okay, Brian— I can see your point. I disliked you before. But I was a teenager with attitude.'

'That's an understatement.'

'Now, now, don't go and spoil it, Brian. I am in two minds as to your true intent, but I will hear you out.'

'So, what can you do?'

'You know what I can do, Brian. You have seen my work, first-hand, haven't you? You've had to clean up the blood and body parts.'

'Tell me everything, Cathy.'

'You never told me— can you be trusted?'

'Yes, I swear.'

'Then we need another coffee. This is a complex tale. Once I have told you, you are no better off as none of it can be proven.'

'I know that. I just need to hear it.'

I gave poor Brian a potted history from cradle to present day. To say he looked overwhelmed was an understatement.

We sat in silence for a good while as he processed all I had told him.

'You still haven't told me why you killed your mother.'

'If I didn't do it, the Darkness would have. He though, would have made her suffer.'

'Why, though?'

'Because he wants me to give myself willingly to him.'

'Why does he want that, other than you are very attractive.'

'Careful Brian. I'm not sure I'm your type.'

'I'd maybe disagree.'

'The Darkness wants me for my powers. He was going to use mum as leverage.'

'So, you killed her?'

'Well, the alternative would be to give in to the Darkness and likely as a consequence, bring about Armageddon.'

'You're that powerful.'

'I would be if I sided with the Darkness. So, what now, Brian?'

'What do you mean what now?'

'I mean— what are your intentions when you leave.'

'I don't have any.'

'I'm sure that's not true. Everyone has an angle, Brian.'

'Okay, maybe.'

'I'm listening. But before you ask, I can't give you the winning numbers for this week's rollover.'

'Do you use your powers at all Cathy?'

'A little where I feel that there is good to be done with them.'

'Well I work missing persons; we have a young girl who disappeared three days ago. We need to find her.'

'You'd like my help to find her?'

'Yes— would you— could you?'

'Of course, I can. It might help me prove to you that I want to use these powers that I have, for good not evil.'

'Are you serious?'

'You couldn't tell anyone about our relationship. But yes, I can help you.'

'Well, I guess we can give it a go.'

'Are you doubting me, Brian, after all I've told you?'

'No, it's just I have not seen you in action apart from you giving me the shits, that was you wasn't it?'

'Yeah— busted— sorry, but I really didn't like you.'

'Fair enough, I wasn't that keen on you either, truth be told.'

'Quits then? So, PC Lyons, what do you know so far?'

'Yeah— don't start that again and its DCI now.'

'Yeah, I know, good for you. You must have been what twenty-five when you came to our house. You must have been a fast-track candidate to be a DC at that age?'

'Yes, I was— on both counts.'

'Do you know what my first thought was when you produced my knickers?'

'That I had you bang to rights—'

I laughed loudly.

'Not quite Brian— I thought, I bet he sniffed them.'

Brian paused, the look on his face said it all.

'Oh my god, you pervert you did—'

NO! — I can't believe you'd even think that.'

'Brian, so it wasn't the look in my eyes that drove you mad all these years but the smell of my panties,' I joked.

'You've got a warped mind, Cathy—'

'I guess your inexperience and naivety were your downfall thinking you'd got me bang to rights.'

'Yes, Cathy— I underestimated you. You are smart— be careful though as that will be your downfall.'

'You'd have to get up pretty early, Brian, if you want to get one over on me.'

'Like I said, that will be your undoing.'

'Anyhow Brian, you hinted earlier that you thought I might be your type.'

'Well you are extremely attractive, Cathy, you always were.'

'Brian, did you fancy me when I was a fourteen-year-old virgin?'

'I could see you would grow up to be a stunner, that's all.'

'Getting defensive Brian— that would have been creepy, but the age gap is less important now, we are both consenting adults.'

Poor Brian did not know what to make of my comments, he knew I liked to yank his chain.

'Like I say— you are a beautiful young woman.'

'Let me be direct then Brian— do you fancy a quickie, because I feel quite horny if I am honest.'

Brian looked like a child being given a free pass to the sweet shop.

'Are you serious?' he asked tentatively.

'Absolutely, Brian— follow me.'

I took Brian upstairs to my bedroom and gave him the ride of his life. He did alright to be fair to him. An hour later, we returned to the lounge, I made another coffee.

'So, Brian, you were about to tell me about a missing person case,' I said.

'Back to business is it, just like that?'

'Brian, please don't read more into it than it was. We fucked. Very nice it was too. It might even happen again. But we are not and nor will we ever be, in a relationship— so yes back to business.'

Brian seemed a little dejected, almost as if he had been used. Maybe he had carried a torch for me for all those years. Perhaps I gave him what he'd wanted and then took it straight back off him. *Men— so fucking complicated.*

'I'm not reading anything into it.'

'Good— so what about this missing person.'

'Well, we have a five-year-old girl named Kerry Williams. She's been missing for three days. She was out playing with friends in the cul-de-sac where she lives. Nobody saw anything.'

'No suspects? No leads whatsoever?'

'Nothing, not even a gut feeling. The parents seem genuine.'

'Okay— let me get in the zone.'

I opened the channels and searched the spiritual ether. The thick soup of souls all wanting to chat. All with a burning message.

'She isn't dead.'

'Really? I figured by now we'd be looking for a body.'

'Do you have anything of hers?'

'Yes! But not with me.'

'I need something she was close to. Better still a lock of hair.'

'Okay, leave it with me. I hope you realise this is a little unorthodox. I shouldn't divulge case information to anyone. But I guess trust goes both ways. When is the best time to catch you?'

'Anytime. I don't venture out much. Well at all, actually. Trust is a big little word, Brian!'

I walked Brian to the door. I think he was hoping for a quick kiss.

'See you soon, I hope,' I said as he left.

He turned and lingered a moment still holding out for a goodbye kiss.

'Count on it,' he replied, as he realised no kiss was going to be forthcoming.

Well, that wasn't what I'd expected when I woke this morning. Another potential positive outlet for my powers and maybe a new friend with benefits.

Chapter 21
Finding Kerry

Brian returned two days later. He had with him Kerry's hairbrush and a recent photograph. What a lovely little girl. The parents were desperate for news. Brian had said he knew a medium and that it must be worth a try; but that they must not speak to the press about it.

I settled into my rhythm and began my search. Like a spiritual sniffer dog.

'Cathy.'

'Mum?'

'Yes, It's me. I can find her for you.'

My mother coming through could be a real time-saver. She knows the drill. I won't get broken fragments that I need to piece together. It will be as if she is sat on my sofa chatting to me in person.

'Okay, that's great.'

'I'll contact you when I have something.'

'Great.'

'Well?' asked Brian enthusiastically.

'Well, it's like doing a google search, just it can take a little longer; we are scouring the whole planet, Brian. Seven and a half billion living souls. Trying to find just one.'

Moments later, my kitchen light flickered.

'Be right back,' I said as I channelled my energy.

'Cathy,'

'Yes mum.'

'Kerry is alive—she has not yet been harmed.'

'Where is she?'

'Strangest thing— I can't pinpoint her.'
'What? Why?'
'She is warded or blocked.'
'The Darkness?'
'Yes! You need to meet the parents. To touch them. To read them.'
'But I can't leave. It may even be a trap.'
'You can resist Cathy. You are in control.'
'Well?' asked, Brian again.
'What do the parents do?' I asked.
'Mr Williams is an accountant. He's a really nice unassuming guy. His wife is a complete contrast. It's clear who wears the trousers in that house. Her father is some property developer.'
'What does she do for a living.'
'Works for daddy, which means she gets paid for doing very little. That's the impression I get at any rate.'
'Spoilt brat?'
'Not so much. She comes over as being quite smart.'
'Good for her.'
'So where are we at? What's our next move?' asked Brian.
'I need to meet them at their home— can you arrange that?'
'Of course. Give me a day or two.'
'Something isn't quite right here, Brian. Keep your wits about you, I fear all is not as it seems.'
'Okay— I'll get on then.'
'Fine, call me to let me know.'
Brian headed out. A man on a mission.
'Mum— you still here.'

'I'm here, Cathy.'

'So, what's going on here. It smells off?'

'I agree, but I can't seem to get close.'

'Who could be doing it— the warding I mean.'

'Well, obviously the Darkness— but maybe another witch.'

'So, it is potentially a trap of some sort?'

'I think it may well be, but the Darkness has nothing to gain. And if it is another witch, the Darkness will protect you. At least that's how I see it.'

'I guess we will know soon enough.'

'Just be on guard.'

'I intend to be. Do you think Kerry is in real danger or just being used as bait?'

'I think she is being used as bait. But I may be wrong. All we know is she is alive for now.'

'Thanks, mum.'

The following day Brian called to say we could meet the parents at their home at 4:00p.m. He would collect me at 3:00p.m. which he duly did.

'Do we know any more Brian?'

'Nope— '

'Great— I take it this is still off book as such.'

'Yup— '

We pulled into the cul-de-sac. Not what I expected.

'Christ Brian, I figured cul-de-sac like a small estate of semi-detached.'

'I know— the father owns the lot. The whole family live here. These are easy a million-plus each.'

'How the other half live. The kidnap must be about money. Surely!'

'No ransom demands. We don't even know if it's a kidnapping.'

'This sort of money often means criminal activity somewhere down the line.'

'Yes, I agree. We can't find anything of substance though.'

'Bloody hell it's a gated community.'

'Yeah, makes it all the more suspicious that Kerry could just disappear like that.'

Brian spoke into the intercom at the main gate, announcing our arrival. The iron gates opened, and we drove to the home of poor little Kerry.

As we alighted the car, Mrs Williams stood at the entrance. Imposing double oak doors guarding the entrance to the palatial home.

Mrs Williams was close to six feet tall. Fire red hair. She was an imposing and attractive woman.

'Good afternoon. You must be Cathy,' she said, presenting her hand to me; 'I'm Valerie.'

'Nice to meet you, Valerie,' I replied as I shook her hand.'

'Hello again, Brian. Please come on in,' she beckoned.

I paused as Brian entered.

'Come on in— both of you,' reiterated Valerie. *Perfect.*

Valerie closed the doors behind us.

'Let's go through to the study,' she said.

We followed her across the vast entrance hall, past a magnificent staircase and into an oak-clad study.

'Take a seat. Is coffee okay with you both?' she asked signalling to a maid as she did.

We both nodded.

'Fine,' we both replied, almost in harmony.

As we waited for the coffee, there was a silence. As I looked around the study, I felt somehow uneasy.

'Will your husband be joining us?' I asked. In an attempt to break the uneasy silence.

'No— but we will be joined by a couple of other people if that's okay?'

'Fine— who?'

At that point, the maid returned with our Coffee. The tray placed on the desk. Adding my sugar and milk, I returned to my seat on one of the large leather sofas.

'Thank you, Marie. You can head home now thank you,' said Valerie to the maid.

'So, shall we get started?' I asked.

'Of course— let me call the others through,' said Valerie, as she opened the study door.

Two men walked in. The first I recognised immediately.

'Paul? What the hell are you doing here?'

'And you remember my brother Todd. He can't walk more than fifty metres without getting out of breath since you gave him a heart condition!'

'What the hell is this? We've been set up,' I said, as I turned to Brian.

Brian rolled his eyes a little.

'Looks that way,' replied Brian.

'Come on we're leaving.'

'Sorry, Cathy, you are not going anywhere,' said Valerie.

'Brian come on let's get out of here,' I again demanded as I rose from my seat.

'Sorry, Cathy,' replied Brian, 'you are going nowhere. Not yet at any rate. Sit down please.'

'What the fuck is this?' I demanded.

Paul stepped forward.

'Cathy, this is revenge. You didn't really think I would just let it go, did you?'

'It seems not— I'd say you've got balls— but you haven't have you?'

'There you go, make your jokes. You won't be laughing when we've all done with you.'

'You know you can't harm me right.'

'Oh, that's right. You're protected by the Darkness. Except this house is warded. Sorry. You're on your own,' replied Paul.

'So, you've planned this carefully— trap sprung. Tell me how did this all come about?'

'Well, as luck or intervention would have it— Todd contacted me to do some ariel photography of a new development. As soon as he saw me; he recognised me.'

'So, you plotted to bring me down?'

'We had a common enemy. You know— my enemies' enemy is my friend. Brian had interviewed Todd after the incident at the bar, he'd made it clear he intended to take you down.'

'You are a sneaky two-faced fucker aren't you Brian. I thought I'd read you. Clearly, I was off, we even fucked!'

Paul shot a look at Brian— Brian shrugged his shoulders dismissively.

'I said your confidence would be your downfall, I guess I must have gotten up pretty fucking early Cathy,' replied Brian, looking quite pleased with himself.

'No, you see Brian was warded too,' said Valerie.

'By who?'

'By me. Who else?'

'You're a witch?'

'Yes— well High Priestess actually— not as powerful as you— but I will be.'

'In your dreams.'

'We'll see.'

'So, Kerry is okay, I assume?'

'She is. She will be returned as a result of sterling police work by DCI Lyons.'

'I guess I should be flattered. This is a lot of trouble. I'm surprised Todd's heart is in it.'

'You will pay for what you have done bitch,' said Todd, speaking for the first time.

'So, how's this going to play out?' I asked.

'You and I are going to splice,' replied Valerie.

'The fuck we are!'

Splicing is a process by which cloning, and transference of powers can be achieved. It requires two people at least one with powers. The second must be in a state of ecstasy at which point the transfer can be completed.

So, in essence, Valerie must be highly aroused and mid-orgasm as it were, I must then at that point transfer the parts of me I wish to share.

'The fuck we will,' said Valerie.

'Or else what. You have nothing to threaten me with.'

'Yes, we have my daughter Kerry. If you refuse, she will die, and we will set you up for her murder. A sick witch using a child's blood to make her spells and potions.'

'You'd kill your own daughter to have my powers?'

'In a flash— Absolutely.'

'What sort of mother are you? That's abhorrent— Where is she?'

'Safe.'

'You do realise that even without the Darkness I can smite you all?'

'We are warded, Cathy. You are powerless in here.'

'Kill your daughter; she is nothing to me. I will beat the charges. I will drop you all in it. You have me all wrong if you think I give a fuck.' I'll t*ry a bluff here to try and remove Kerry as leverage.*

'My daughter dies, and so do you. Remember the Darkness can't save you.'

'Look I know it is possible for almost anyone to learn black magic. It is like anything else; you can teach someone to be competent at art or hairstyling. But without natural talent. You will never be the top of your game. I am the result of five-hundred years of genetic manipulation. You are nothing.'

'Well we will see how good I am, won't we. I managed to trap you.'

'I expect you have never been in direct contact with the Darkness. Maybe some of his minions but you and your coven have never spoken to the Darkness have you.'

'So?'

'Well, had you done; You would know he would not approve of this. You are acting against your Dark Lords own interests. What do you think he is going to do when he learns of your betrayal?'

'I don't need his permission. Once I have your powers, he will want me by his side.'

'No— you're already out of your depth Val!'

'You are good with words, Cathy. Always ready with a witty or sarcastic response. But it is you who is out of your depth now,' interjected Paul.

'So, can we be clear. So, I know for sure that you intend to kill me and poor little Kerry if I refuse to splice with ginger spice over there?'

'That about sums it up,' replied Todd.

'And Brian, as an officer of the law, you are going to be accessory to double homicide?'

'If that's what it takes to bring you down, you cocky little bitch.'

'Seems you have me bang to rights.'

'Outwitted you're not as clever as you thought are you, Cathy?' Said, Paul.

'I will save you until last Paul.'

'Big words from an impotent witch.'

'You're the only impotent fool in this room, Paul. Then we've got the tin man over there. I bet If I shout boo too loud, he'll drop dead.'

'You are screwed, Cathy. Just splice and make this easy on everyone,' said Brian.

'Look, guys, you are all amateurs. You've tried hard and planned well I will give you that. But as always, you have underestimated me and my little friend the Darkness. Do you think you can try and fuck him over without serious consequences? He wants and needs me. He has no interest in some spliced cheap imitation. He created me. Five hundred years in the making. You are all fucked. So last chance. Cut me loose and free Kerry. I will only offer it once.'

'You are good. I'll give you that. You almost had me there. You must be a good poker player. I can't spot a single tell on your face,' said Valerie.

'There is no tell Val. Because I am not lying.'

Paul knew me well enough to know I was serious. Brian and Todd thought I was bluffing and Val. Well, she was mulling it over.

'Guy's, I think she might be telling the truth,' said Paul hesitantly.

'That's what she wants you to think,' replied Todd.

'Deal or no deal guy's— who the fuck is in charge anyway?'

'I am!' replied Val— 'No deal.'

There was a moment of uneasy silence.

'Okay— so I figured this was indeed some kind of set up. I knew warding had been used because my dear old dead mum told me. I have warding on my own home it is very effective indeed.'

'Yes, it is impenetrable,' said Val arrogantly.

'Well, almost Val.'

Val laughed.

'It is bulletproof— I thought you were good,' said Val, assuredly.

'I am better than good Val. Unfortunately, you are not. Which is why you are doomed to fail.'

'How do you figure?'

'Well, I knew you had warding; very good warding. I knew this was likely a trap. So much as I hated having to do it. I contacted the Darkness. He confirmed this was all a ruse and that it had nothing to do with him.'

At this point, the atmosphere changed slightly from a smug satisfaction to nervous anticipation.

'Given that; — my protector and arguably my tormentor— hitched a ride. He was already with me when we arrived here and you Val dear— You invited him in! — that renders your warding as effective as a chocolate fireguard.'

'She's still bluffing,' said Todd.

'You're not the sharpest knife in the drawer are you, Todd? —'

'Fuck you, bitch.'

'Say hello to my little friend—' I said in my best Al Pacino voice. *I love that film*.

They all looked at me, waiting for it. Not sure whether to attack me where I sat. Run for the hills or simply accept their fate.

'Told you she's all Talk,' said Todd.

But It's all about timing. Paul knew it.

Now I had done more than let the Darkness in. I had allowed him to take over my body. Giving him seven hours on board actual possession. The way it works is that I get fifty-three minutes and fifty-four seconds at the helm, he gets six hours, six minutes and six seconds, to do what he wants.

This deal usually ends in the death of the donor body. But for me, it's more of a loss leader. I might enjoy what I can do. I might become intoxicated by the enormity of my power. I might say yes to the Darkness. Either way, this is a onetime never to be repeated event.

The Beauty of this is that the devil takes the rap. Even if I kill an innocent while possessed, it does not get chalked up to my account.

Okay, let's play.

I got up from the sofa and looked around the room, deciding who should be first. Todd bottled it and tried to open the doors to the study. The doors were not going to open, Not yet; as he tugged and rattled the door handle.

'Sorry, Todd— too late. I gave you all the chance to do the right thing. Something that I always do. You didn't choose to take me up on it and so now— well now you will pay for that.'

'What do you intend to do to us? asked Todd as he finally gave up on trying to open the door.

'Well, it's a tough call. I am a truly nice person. But I have a vengeful streak. It rises up, and it punishes as Paul and Todd can both attest.'

'Well if all you can do is lock a door. I'm not sure we need to worry too much,' said Brian.

'Brian, you did not as you seem to think; get up anywhere near early enough to get one over on me— you will be sorry.'

'We'll see,' replied Brian dismissively.

'Can I just say before we get started. You are currently all stood in a room with the single most powerful being on the planet. Seven and a half billion people. All creatures great and small. I am the Apex. They say that power corrupts, and that absolute power corrupts absolutely. I can certainly see how that might be so. I could vaporise you all. I could tear off your limbs one by one. I could strike you down in countless ways. I feel intoxicated by it. But if I do succumb, I know that I will never come back from it.'

'And yet all you've done is locked a door,' Brian once again noted defiantly.

'What? Do you want a demo, do you, Brian?' I said as I turned to face him.'

Brian was sat in an armchair. The study was large. A Brazilian mahogany desk dominated the room. A stag's head on the wall. High-end furniture. Cut crystal drink decanters. In fact, all the expected trappings of someone playing rich man; with dirty money.

As I looked at Brian, I simply pointed at him with my right index finger. He immediately started to choke as if being strangled. He stood from his chair and clutched his throat in an attempt to remove the invisible hands that were choking the life from him. As I released him, he fell back into the chair.

'How was that, Brian?'

I turned to Todd, who was stood beneath the stag's head.

'Or I can be the reanimator,' I said, as the Stag suddenly grunted loudly. Todd jumped half out of his skin. 'Careful Todd, you nearly had a heart attack there old boy.'

While I was distracted, Val had opened the desk drawer where she had surreptitiously hidden a knife. She came at me from behind. Ready to bring the blade down in the back of my neck.

I turned, as she wrestled to stick the knife in me. Her hand held in mid-air. Unable to move.

'You are a back-stabbing little bitch, aren't you Val?' I said.

I took the knife from her hand.

'My word Val. Do you know what this is?'

'It's a ceremonial blade.'

'No— it isn't Val, it is the blade of Nalvage the pursuer of beasts.'

'It's what?'

'What is it doing in your grubby little mitt's?'

'I paid a small fortune for it.'

'I bet you did. But it's priceless! You do not know its power— in the right hands that is. Not in yours.'

'It's for making sacrifices.'

'No, Val. You see a little knowledge is a dangerous thing. It will kill evil. By that it means demons, but moreover. It kills evil people like you.'

'Any knife can do that.'

'Yes, but this one kills your soul.'

'What?'

'Yes, it destroys your soul. No heaven, no hell, no rebirth— gone forever.'

'The soul cannot be destroyed. You are the one who is misinformed.'

'No, it can't be destroyed. It is wiped clean and the energy absorbed by the holder of the knife. Tell me then. You believed that stabbing me would kill both me and the Darkness. That's not very nice now is it Val.'

'Fuck you!'

'I think we have established just who is in charge here,' I said, 'I'm not bluffing. I think we all agree on that at least.'

'So, get on with it, bitch,' spat Val.

'You all conspired to lure me here on the pretext of saving a little girl— your own daughter Val. And you tell me you were willing to kill her to get your way.'

'We were bluffing. I'd never hurt my daughter.'

'Yes, you would! — you wanted my powers for your own ends, and you intended to kill me either way.'

'I'm a police officer. They will lock you up and throw away the key if you kill me,' expounded Brian.

'You are a disgrace to the badge, Brian. You have no idea what I have in store for you. But we'll get to it in due course— so— who wants to go first?'

The room fell silent. The tension was tangible as they all looked to one another, each hoping that someone would step forward.

'Look, I punish according to the crime. Some of you might argue I do this disproportionately. I would say my punishments always fit the crime. So— knowing this, I am going to give you all a chance. Based on your crimes; you must choose an appropriate punishment. If I agree that it is both appropriate and adequate, I will administer it. That will be an end to it. If not, I will choose my own. Think carefully based on your knowledge of my past punishments— if you try and lowball me with some pathetic affliction, I will kill you outright. I'll give you a moment to consider.'

They all looked as though they were waiting to be hung. In many ways, that is precisely the effect I had desired. The Darkness was enjoying this. Torment is his game, and he loved this.

'If any of you have seen the *Saw* films. You probably get the drift,' I added.

Knowing your crimes. Recognising your wrongs. Accepting responsibility for your actions. It's never easy, is it? Choosing a just punishment that will save your life but leave very obvious scars is almost impossible— the alternative. Death!

Okay then— Todd— you're first up.'

I was half expecting the pressure to give him a fatal heart attack. It didn't.

'Todd what would be appropriate for you? You plotted to catch and kill me, to force me to give my powers to your sister and to be an accessory in the murder of your own niece. What I wonder do you think I should do to you— and before we start— if anyone's opening statement is along the lines of *please don't do this*— I will kill you on the spot— good we're all clear then.'

'Well given that your previous punishment has left me like this, anything more would leave me completely useless. I was wrong to do what I did. I let anger and vengeance drive me. As such I say, please just kill me and have done with it. That is what I deserve.'

Well, I wasn't expecting that. Though he is, of course, correct.

'Wow— Tod— You caught me off guard with that one. I didn't think you had it in you. I could argue though that for you, death is the easy option. But then by my own rules, I would have to punish you by death— what to do? — You clearly love your sister Todd.'

'Yes— very much.'

'Well, I tell you what. You have warmed my heart with your honesty. I am going to restore your health for you. Let you feel once more how it feels to be a healthy young man.

And then, as for your punishment. I will come back to that later.'

I walked over to Todd and restored his health. Something I was able to do only using the powers of the Darkness. Todd was instantly restored. Colour back in his face.

'Feels good, does it Todd?'

'Thank you.'

'Don't thank me just yet. Just consider which life you would prefer.'

'Now Val— I suspect you are the brains behind this. You craved my powers. You were willing to murder your own daughter to get them. You tried to kill me and the Darkness by stabbing us in the back. What I wonder do you consider an apt punishment for such crimes?'

'Well, my lust for power was my undoing. I was blinded and corrupted by the thought of having such powers as yours. You should take all of my powers from me,' replied Val hesitantly.

'Yes— I thought you might say that. Your powers are fair; not great. You didn't get what you wanted, which was my power. So, in effect, you would really not be much worse off now without any powers at all. You intended to kill your daughter.'

'But you would be stripping me of the one thing I love; my power.'

'Valerie— you would really have killed Kerry? You told us she was bait,' said Todd; who was seemingly as disgusted as I was at Val's callous nature.

'Oh— be quiet, Todd,' spat Val.

'No, the one thing you love Val is you,' I replied.

'Todd— would you like to keep the new revitalised you or return to chronic angina and not being able to walk fifty metres without a rest?'

I didn't need to ask the question; it was pretty obvious.

'The new me. I want this.'

'Good— then to keep it; the remainder of your sentence is to kill your sister.'

'What?' Shouted Todd as he shot a look at his sister.

'You heard me. She just said the one thing she loves is her power. Not you. Not Kerry. I will kill her if you don't. If you don't, I will fuck up your heart again. Your choice.'

The atmosphere changed again. Adrenalin was now coursing through everyone. This was like gladiatorial games the spectators getting fired up; waiting for the battle to commence. The two gladiators preparing to fight. Preparing to die.

You might have expected total pandemonium. Hysterical pleas for mercy. But assembled before me was Paul. Paul knew from first-hand experience my capabilities without the power-up I'd received from the Darkness. Todd was a recipient of my previous smiting. Brian had previously cleaned up the blood and body parts from my exploits in revenge. Val. Well, Val was a hard-faced callous woman; willing to murder her own daughter and me. They knew that crying and begging for mercy would get them nothing but a torturous end.

'Val— if you manage to kill your brother, I will let you live and give you my powers. How's that for a game-changer?'

'You're fucking Sick,' said Paul.

'Maybe I am. But let's not forget why I am here in the first place. So, the first question is— Todd— do you accept my punishment?'

'No— I'm not playing your stupid fucking games. I won't kill my sister. Despite what she has said and done today. I love her. You are sick and twisted,' replied Todd. Looking like he might actually start to cry.

'Hold that thought, Todd. And don't you dare cry— Val the deal still stands will you fight Todd regardless?'

Val grabbed the knife from the desk, where I had placed it. She lunged for Todd without a word of warning. Seems my powers were all she cared about.

Todd dodged her first thrust and planted a powerful right hook to her head. Val staggered back as Todd grabbed her right hand to wrestle the knife from her. They tussled for a while. toing and froing. Todd was strong. But Val was determined.

Eventually, Todd wrestled Val to the floor. Sat astride her he turned the knife, still in her hand, towards her throat.

'Why Val? I didn't want to do this,' said Todd.

The tip of the blade was now pressing into her neck. The skin pierced and a little blood oozing from the wound. Todd waited momentarily. He had both physical and mechanical advantage. Applying just a fraction more pressure would end his sister's life.

'What are you waiting for Todd?' I asked.

'I can't kill her— I won't kill her,' replied Todd.

He got up from on top of Val. The knife in his hand. Val gave a massive sigh of relief as she picked herself up from the floor. A smug, satisfied look on her face.

'You really are testing me, Todd. You continue to surprise me. Your sister would have killed you. Even after you refused to fight her. Yet you still spared her life.'

'She is my sister, and I love her.'

'Give me the knife, Todd.'

Todd reluctantly did as instructed.

'Okay, Todd, you stand there and do not move a fucking muscle. Is that clear?'

Todd nodded.

'Here Val. The deal still stands. Just walk over there and cut Todd's throat,' I said as I handed her the knife.

I wanted to test her loyalties one last time. Give her a chance to do the right thing.

Val looked at the blade. She looked at Todd. Without a moment's hesitation, she lunged at Todd's throat. I stopped her. Now frozen to the spot I took the knife from her.

'So, your brother refuses to fight you, then when he has the chance, refuses to kill you and yet you still put my powers before such love and devotion?'

'You made a deal,' said Val. Seemingly confused as to why I had stopped her.

'Well, yes. But Todd spared you. I was hoping that you would now do the right thing and take your punishment, but you are truly ruthless and completely heartless.'

'What are you going to do to me?' she asked.

'Well, I was going to make you look like a haggard old witch, give you a wart or two on your face; blacken some teeth and make you look like you're ninety years old.'

'What?' she gasped.

'Don't worry— I said was— No I'm just going to kill you instead,' I replied.

The knife in my hand entered her abdomen in an upward direction. The blade was a foot long curved slightly with a polished bone handle and a silver hilt. I lifted her from the floor. Her hands grasped my arm and hilt of the knife. The blade cut through her as her weight pulled her further down its razor-sharp edge. I just had to kill this evil bitch with my own hands; and not by using my powers. I needed to look her in the eye as I ended her. I yanked out the knife. Several feet of her intestines erupted from the wound. She dropped to the floor; blood running from the wound as I stood with the knife in my hand. She would die slowly of blood loss and asphyxia as her diaphragm had also been punctured; the pool of blood growing by the second as she groaned. She clutched her wound, in a futile attempt to stem the blood loss. Her intestines laid across her abdomen.

I felt the surge of power travel through the blade and into me. This was a permanent power-up. It would significantly increase my powers. The rush it gave me was indescribable.

'Right she's dead—' I announced coldly.

The room was again deathly quiet. The remaining three players stood in stunned silence wondering what was to be.

'Todd— don't look so sad. She was going to kill you. You really have restored my faith. Even though technically, you did not do as I requested. I will spare you.'

'So, what now?' asked Todd.

'Well you can sit down, maybe you can be a juror. So, one down, one spared, two to go— Brian, you're up next. What do you deem a just punishment for your misdeeds?'

Silence.

'Come on, Brian, don't be shy.'

'You are a power-drunk bitch, I'm not going to play your stupid fucking game.'

'Are you sure you want to do it like this, Brian? If you're smart, you might even redeem yourself like Todd did.'

'Okay! — You thought you were smarter than me ten years ago. I wanted to show you that you weren't— clearly, I was wrong. They say that pride comes before a fall and so here I am.'

'Yeah— nice speech but what about the consequences. You tricked me into believing in you. I thought you were a friend.'

'Then put a curse on me so that I will never know love and never have a single friend for the rest of my days.'

'That's actually pretty good, Brian. What do you think, Todd?'

'He's a copper he probably doesn't have many friends anyway,' replied Todd.

'That's possibly a little harsh there Todd. You're not a fan of the police I take it. But this is Brian, your partner in crime. Do you think that would be an appropriate punishment?'

'No, I don't, to be honest.'

'I would tend to agree with you, Todd. You see, Brian's crimes are many. Apart from being a willing accomplice to kidnap— potential double murder and betraying a friend. He also broke his oath to serve and protect.'

'That's the American oath,' interrupted Brian.

'It's really not the time to be nit-picking, Brian.'

'Listen to yourself— who the fuck do you think you are? — just fucking smite me, it's what you do best you murderous hypocritical cunt.'

'Really Brian— such a dirty mouth— sticks and stones Brian.'

'How do you think you're going to get away with this?' replied Brian.

'Todd, where is Kerry?' I asked.

'At my house. In the basement; blindfolded.'

'You look like a family who probably owns guns. Am I correct?'

'No.'

'Todd, I thought we were friends now. Wax jackets, Harris tweed. A stag's head for fuck's sake. Don't you dare try and play me now.'

'Okay— Yes, we have shotguns.'

'What about security cameras?'

'We don't have them. The type of people we do business with don't like their pictures being taken.'

'Not even hidden cameras Todd. You seem the type of family who would collect information for blackmail purposes?'

'Yes, but only in my dad's place— I swear.'

'Finally, what about cash. How much do you have in the safe?'

'A quarter of a million maybe.'

'Well go and fetch a loaded gun, will you? Also, bring the cash in a holdall or rucksack and bring Kerry. Keep her blindfolded. Don't speak to her. Lock her in a bedroom upstairs— and Todd.'

'What?'

'Do not even think about fucking me over.'

'I'm not fucking stupid.'

'And yet here we are.'

Todd returned within ten minutes. Exacting revenge is one thing. Getting away with it is entirely something else.

'Okay, Todd I want you to shoot and Kill Brian.'

'What?'

'Just do it.'

'Todd— don't listen to her you need me alive, to get us all out of this pickle. Kill me, and you're screwed,' said Brian, as he approached Todd nervously.

'No, you see you kidnapped Kerry. You asked for a ransom and came to collect. Val tried to kill you for taking her daughter. You fought, and you stabbed her. Todd heard the screams and ran over to find you with the knife in your hands and the money on the table. He shot you.'

'And what about Paul over there?' asked Brian.

'Don't you worry about Paul. His presence doesn't fit in here. I have other plans for him. You can make that story work, can't you Todd? Obviously, the truth would make you look like some crackpot and likely mean that they prosecute you for double murder.'

'I can make that work,' replied Todd, with commitment.

'Shoot him then.'

Brian walked toward Todd. Maybe hoping if he looked him in the eyes that Todd wouldn't be able to pull the trigger. Perhaps he wanted to get close enough to disarm him— He did get close— Todd shot Brian. Those things make a real mess at close range. Bits of Brian's skull and brain dripped down the wall behind him. His face completely obliterated. His lifeless body laid on the floor.

'Okay, Todd, I need to plant some fake memories in poor Kerry's head. She will be able to vividly describe Brian and the fact she was kept in a garage somewhere. Wipe the knife handle clean and place it in Brian's hand— His left hand; he was a lefty. It's all in the detail, Todd. Women usually stab in a downward stroke but as you saw I stabbed Val in an upward thrust, just as a man would do—'

'Should I be disturbed that you know that? —'

'I guess not— Now, I have given you a chance, Todd. I do believe you are a changed man. Your niece will need you now that her mother is gone. Be clear the Darkness wanted you dead. Don't make me regret this. When I leave, call the police. Do not even mention my name. Are we clear?

'Yes— Just go.'

'Right Paul, I guess your car is out front, is it?'

'Yes— '

'So, let's go, shall we? Back to your place I think.'

We walked down to Paul's car.

'Cathy—' Paul started.

'Just get in the fucking car Paul— and shut your treacherous mouth or I swear—'

Chapter 22
The Journey Back to Paul's

'Looks as though I'm alone with my thoughts for half an hour as she doesn't look as though she intends to speak.'

'What the fuck is she going to do to me?' *Fuck me up, that's what.*

'Maybe I crash the car and hope I either kill her or at least injure her. I can go on the run.'

She'd only find me. Or I'd spend the rest of my life looking over my shoulder.

Can't believe they suckered me into this. Fucking Brian. Glad he's dead. *What a fucking mess I'll never sleep again.*

'This is fucking messed up. I've just watched the woman I love slaughter another fucking witch and have a police officer shot in the fucking face.' *I'm a witness, I'm a dead man.*

Shit, she is going to kill me.

'Should I try and talk her down?' *No, she told me to shut up. She meant it.*

'I wonder if she still has any feelings for me. We had five years together, it has to mean something.' *Yeah. I did fuck Linda though— that fucking bitch. Oh, and I just tried to set her up with ginger witch.*

God, I wish they'd spliced that would have been so fucking hot, ginger witch was a real MILF and boy can Cathy fuck.' *Fucks sake what am I even thinking that for, I'm about to die?*

'She did seem calm back there. Cold-hearted but calm. Ruthless but calm, calm, that's good.' *But she killed them anyway.*

'Maybe I try the Todd approach and say she should kill me'. *She won't go for it she has something much worse in store for me. I know what she'll do.*

'Bitch is probably reading my thoughts.' *Bitch!*

'Fuck did she just look at me and smirk.' *Fuck it!*

'I still fucking love her though.' *She fucking hates me I know it. She said she'd save me until last.*

'I can't believe Todd. I'd have killed Val without a second thought evil bitch. She told us that Kerry was the bait and would not be hurt. Lying bitch— lying dead bitch.' *Fuck Cathy lifted her in the air like a fucking ragdoll.*

She still looks fucking angry. She'll take her time with me. I can't imagine the shit she's going to do to me.

'Only five more minutes and we're there. I won't see tomorrow.' *Maybe I deserve it? I betrayed her— twice. They were going to kill her, and I helped them. I had to be there what a prick. I had to gloat that we got her. That we were smarter than she was. FUCK!*

'I wonder if I'll get a last wish. I'd love to fuck her one more time.' *Maybe she could fuck me to death. That I could die for.*

'Here we are.' *FUCK! I need a drink.*

Chapter 23
I Hate You. Sorry. Thanks

Forty minutes later, we arrived at Pauls apartment. The journey had been torturously silent. *For him, not me.*

Paul opened the door; throwing his keys on the side as we entered.

'Do you want a drink Cathy?' he asked.

'Paul! I am now technically on Darkness time. However, he is letting me run over on the meter. I think he is curious as to how this will play out. He wants to see if his faith in me is well placed I guess.'

'Drink— yes or no?'

'I'll have a whiskey— you know how I take it.'

Paul poured two large whiskeys and added a splash of water.

'Cheers,' he said as he took a gulp.

'So, Paul, what should your punishment be?'

'Just kill me, Cathy.'

'That was Todd's trump card. You can't use it. He meant it, you don't.'

'You're going to take my eyes, Cathy, aren't you? I know how your mind works.'

'Why did you come after me, Paul?'

'I hated you. Not for what you did. But for why. I made a judgement; Linda was going to try and ruin what we had. I was wrong, but I did it to protect you; not to hurt you. But you punished me anyway. Everything is so black or white with you. '

'You slept with my sister.'

'I love you, Cathy, I always will. The biggest punishment is not having you. Not being close to you. Not being loved by you. Anything else that you do to me is insignificant by comparison. I live every day wishing that I could undo what I did. I know I betrayed your trust, and it kills me a little more each day.'

'Then why were you with those people who were plotting to kill me?'

'I got consumed with vengeance. You of all people must understand that.'

'Ouch!'

'Truth hurts doesn't it Cathy.'

'I am sorry, Paul. I acted in anger, and it was too late to undo what I had done. I, too, have been tortured by what I did. I wanted many times to call you to make things right. But how can I make right what I did to you?'

'I forgive you, Cathy. I understand your constant torment. It's not too late to make it better.'

I pondered what Paul was saying. I did still love him. He clearly still loved me, and he was right. I intended to take his sight from him.

'Paul, I need time to think. But I won't take your sight. Obviously, what has happened today needs to stay our secret.'

'That goes without saying, Cathy. So, what now?'

'I'm going home— that's what, call me a cab while I shower and change— I assume you still have some of my things.'

'Of course— I never stopped hoping you'd come back.'

I showered and changed; finished my Whiskey and turned to leave. Paul walked me to the door; as I reached to open it, I turned to kiss him.

As our lips met, both of my hands were suddenly around his neck. As they squeezed, he managed to say; 'Cathy, what are you doing?'

'This is no longer Cathy. She is clearly not ready to give herself to me. Maybe this will help with her decision making. She is in here watching you die.'

The Darkness was driving now. The pressure applied crushed Paul's neck, like a packet of crisps; Collapsing his windpipe; and bursting blood vessels in his eyes, he was dead in seconds. As the grip was released, he fell to the floor.

We turned and left.

'You were so close Cathy. Your performance earlier was simply sublime, and you did it without resorting to the use of your powers. Sadly, it does seem as though you are not quite ready to give yourself to me. Paul had to die. You know that.'

'So, what sort of rampage are we going on; now that you have time left to kill as it were.'

'Well, it was all a bit short notice. I have no plans. If I were in a man's body, I'd probably just hit the red-light district. I like to do the fucking. Not get fucked, if you know what I mean?'

I got out of the cab and walked up my garden path to my front door.

'So, we're done.'

'You're not going to invite me in for Coffee then Cathy?'

'Nice try— and I guess— although it sticks in my throat— a thank you is in order. I'd be dead had you not offered this solution.'

'I was never going to let that happen, Cathy— five hundred years in the making only to die at the hands of halfwits and wannabes.'

'Were you not tempted to let me splice with Val? As I'm sure, she would have jumped at the chance to be your sidekick.'

'No— she would have had the breadth of your powers— but not the strength. Plus, she did make some rooky mistakes— you're much smarter. I need a thinker like you Cathy, you are a cunning little fucker I will give you that.'

'I hate you for what you did to Paul. He didn't have to die.'

'It was quick. You know in your heart he had to die, but you couldn't do it.'

'It was my choice to let him be. You had no business killing him.'

'You can't afford to show weakness, Cathy. Paul conspired against you. He would have seen you die if Val had her way. You let things like that cloud your vision. You must have absolute clarity of vision and purpose. You let Michael live, and he came after you. You need to be decisive. You must learn to kill those who stand against you. Show no mercy. No compassion and no forgiveness. Give no quarter. You know that.'

'But I loved Paul, despite what he did. Is that weakness or empathy?'

'Same thing. And that Cathy will be your downfall.'

'Or my salvation.'

'I suggest you think carefully about just what it is that I would consider to be your downfall.'

'You will never have me.'

'Well, let's wait and see. If you're not inviting me in— I'll be on my way. And it's so rare I get an outing. You did me proud today, Cathy. Until the Paul incident at least— but I won't hold it against you. I left you a power upgrade by the way. I guess you'll see what it is when you need it.'

As I turned the key in my lock, the Darkness was gone.

I poured a glass of wine; and flopped on my couch.

My thoughts returned to Paul. Maybe we could have made things work. He was a good man. His mistake though. Not sleeping with Linda. No. His mistake was that he ever met me. That he ever bought me a drink in the bar the night we first met. His mistake was that he thought he saw the good in me. I cried a little as I remembered the good times we'd shared. I then locked all of those thoughts and emotions safely away. Weakness! That's all they are.

I flicked the TV on— there was breaking news.

The news was reporting that missing child Kerry Williams had been returned safe and well and that the chief investigating officer appeared to be implicated. He had killed the child's mother before being shot dead by her brother.

The chief of police commented that; *'there appears to have been a complex kidnap and ransom plot against a wealthy family, who are pillars of the community? We are unable to provide further details at the moment as our investigations continue. Though at this time, we are not looking for any other persons in relation to this crime.'*

I wondered how long Paul's body would lay undiscovered. I have a life full of regrets. This one though was at the top of the list. I'd loved this man. He had loved me. I had no right to do what I did. Linda should be the one who is dead. She got what she wanted in the end. I took the bait and acted on impulse. I did this to myself. *Act in haste repent at leisure.* I see now why wrath is one of the seven deadly sins. It not only hurts the intended recipient but the giver too. Does any good really come of it? Momentary quenching of the thirst that is vengeance. But the thirst does not remain sated for long, as that which quenches quickly sours.

Chapter 24
Case closed?

It had undoubtedly been an eventful few weeks since I had last heard from Steph. She was doing her undercover work. I had killed my mum and three other people directly or indirectly since we'd last met.

I would keep that from her for now. Apart from my mother's death. Steph deserved to know that.

There seemed to have been no apparent fallout from the death of DCI Lyons and his conspirators, so that was a relief. Todd had clearly kept it together. The news update said he was being charged with manslaughter and was entering a plea of diminished responsibility. Presumably, as he'd walked in to find his sister stabbed to death; along with the pressure and stress already caused by the kidnap of his niece; finding a policeman holding the knife in one hand and a bag of cash in the other it would be argued that this had tipped Todd over the edge.

'Come on in Steph— It's great to see you,' I said as I greeted her in the usual manner.

'You're looking well, Cathy— how are things.'

'Well, I lost my mum shortly after we last met. It was quick. It happened here. A heart attack.'

'Oh— Cathy— I'm sorry. Come here, give us a hug.'

'I'm okay— really. I get to speak to her, so I know she's in a good place.'

'It must make all the difference, knowing absolutely that there is something after this life.'

'It does— so what's been happening with your current story?'

'Well I obviously got the job— the boss is definitely an ass man,' Laughed Steph, they all call him Steady Eddie. He is a smooth operator. But not the type you'd want to mess with. I get the impression he was sleeping with the previous secretary. I think he'd like to do the same with me. I can use that.'

'So, have you managed to find much out? Apart from him having a cool nickname and designs on your ass.'

'Are you a little Jealous Cathy.'

'Concerned I think would be more accurate,' I replied with a grin.

'I know when the next shipment is due. Customs are going to do a small test drilling into the box section and see if it is loaded with cocaine. If it is, they will let it be collected and then raid them when they start to dismantle the machinery to extract the drugs.'

'How will they know when that is going to be?'

'I need to try and find out how quickly they extract the drugs. I guess they will do it at night as there would be less chance of casual disturbance.'

'That would make sense. Why can't they just raid them when the plant is delivered?'

'Because they could quite rightly say that they didn't know it was in there.'

'I suppose. The old technicality strikes again. Even though any right-minded person can see what the score is. It's not enough in court.'

'Precisely.'

'So, what's your plan.'

'I don't have one— I just need to keep snooping. I will know when it gets delivered. And the police and customs will be ready at short notice. But the timing must be perfect.'

'How about this then. We ask Graham if he can watch the hanger and he can alert me when they turn up to extract the drugs. I can alert you, and you can do what you need to do.'

'That sounds too easy.'

'You'd rather do it the hard way and get caught, would you?'

'I guess not. Can you really do that?'

'You're not back to being a doubter are you Steph.'

'No— Maybe you should become a police officer. Your crime detection rates would be off the charts.'

'The problem is most of my suspects would likely meet an untimely demise as I'm not sure I could contain my wrath; not faced with some of the horrors that go on out there.'

'Maybe a vigilante then.'

'Maybe,' I laughed. 'Go make a coffee Steph I will try and contact Graham.'

Steph headed to the kitchen. I contacted Graham. I eventually managed to work through it with him. He was challenging to communicate with as such a newly deceased soul. I said he should practice trying to contact me; rather than waiting for me to reach out to him. This would be imperative if we were to catch them red-handed.

'Okay— so Graham is going to practice contacting me, and he will keep watch for us. When is the shipment due?'

'Tuesday. It then goes into holding until customs clear it. If it has drugs, they will contact me to give the green light. Delivery should then be Thursday or Friday depending on the availability of hauliers.'

'Wow—so close.'

'You get the scoop, do you?'

'Of course, as well as taking some credit for the bust.'

'Good for you,' I replied.

'You mentioned about the horrors out there earlier.'

'Yes, there are some dreadful acts committed.'

'Yes. Working on this case, I missed the whole Williams kidnapping. Did you see it on the news?' Asked Steph.

'Yes, I did— it said the copper was corrupt in the end?'

My contact says he was squeaky clean as far as they knew. No red flags or anything. They said the brother had blown his head clean off. Apparently, he seems quite disturbed and is currently sectioned.'

'I guess that would do that to you. Finding your sister murdered by a kidnapping copper.'

'My contact reckons there is something that doesn't quite stack up. But it's more a gut feeling than anything else.'

'It must have been an awful scene. I hope the poor little girl was not privy to any of it.'

'No, she gave a detailed description of her abductor. It was the officer to a tee.'

'Open and shut case then surely?'

'It would seem so. The only thing that doesn't figure is that Kerry was blindfolded. Yet she had clearly seen her abductors face. So, what's the point of the blindfold?' puzzled Steph.

'Maybe so that she couldn't describe where exactly she had been.'

'I guess so. But she said she had been kept in a garage.'

'Guess we'll never know; as everyone except the brother is dead. And it sounds as though he won't be much use to anyone for a while,' I said.

'True.'

'What are your plans for the rest of the day Steph?'

'I have a few loose ends to sort out. Back to work tomorrow and hopefully by the end of the week, this will all be done and dusted.'

'We should celebrate once we've put it all to rest.'

'Definitely. I'd better get on— great to see you, Cathy. And again— I'm so sorry to hear about your mum. Take care.'

'Yeah— you too.'

I locked the door behind her. Walking back to my armchair, I pondered her remarks. I had left a tiny clue. Unintentional. The blindfold was an oversight. Hopefully, Steph would not be looking to stick her nose in. Todd was a potential loose cannon. The Darkness was right. I showed weakness in letting him live.

Then there was Paul. Nothing on the news. He must be rotting well by now. The Darkness could have made it look like natural causes. Instead, it is now clearly a murder case. What I wonder will they consider the motive. My name will undoubtedly be in the mix. The recently separated long term girlfriend who caught her fiancé in bed with her sister. Yes, Linda was a loose end too. She could stir the pot and likely would. This could become a very tangled web indeed. *Do I let it play out? Do I take pre-emptive and decisive action? I knew what the Darkness would advise. Maybe my killing spree was not yet over! If they stand against me, they will perish.*

Chapter 25
The Big Day Arrives

So precisely as anticipated, the plant machinery arrived at the docks as scheduled. Customs did indeed find cocaine within the structure. The machine was loaded and sent for delivery.

Graham had initially struggled to break through to me if I was not channelling at the time. He had now got the hang of it. I knew we were close. I tried to stay loosely connected as much as I could to make it easier for him.

It was just gone midnight on Friday. Graham came through to me.

'It's happening now,' he said.

I texted Steph to let her know.

It was gone 4:00a.m. when my phone rang; it was Steph.

'We got them, Cathy—said Steph excitedly, 'the raid was a total success. Armed police stormed the building. They arrested six people at the site, including Eddie.'

'That's great news. What now. What about the bent copper and the man who shot Graham?'

'They reckon that Eddie will talk. Faced with the charges, he will want to do a deal. As yet though we don't know just what he will give up.'

'That's good news though Steph. You must be pleased it's all over?'

'I am. Need to find something else to get my teeth, or should I say our teeth into.'

'I will look out for the story in the Gazette.'

'Nationals— this one is going national; it is potentially the biggest cocaine seizure in ten years.'

'Wow— you're going to be sought after. But with that comes unwanted attention from the likes of Eddie and his associates. You must be careful Steph.'

'I will be. I will pop in to see you late next week— got to go— bye.'

'Bye.'

The following week; Wednesday, Steph, as promised, called in to update me.

'Cathy—Steady Eddie has rolled over on who killed Graham. He claims he told the man to warn him not to kill him. Both men have been arrested. So, they have Grahams killer. Isn't that fantastic?'

'That is fab. What about that bent copper?'

'No joy. He denies even knowing him.'

'Maybe we make him our next person of interest Steph. Nothing worse than a bent copper.'

'You read my mind.'

'No, I didn't— honest,' I joked.

Steph laughed.

'So, what now?' asked Steph.

'Let me see if Graham is near.'

I managed to contact him and asked if he now had a message for his wife and son. He did. It was standard fare, to be honest. I guess though it is what people need and want to hear. His message:

Tell my wife that I will always love her. That I will always be there with her. That I miss her, even her smelly feet. Tell her to tell my son Liam to always be true to himself and that I will be watching over him too.

I relayed the message to Steph to pass on to Graham's wife and reiterated that she does not mention me by name.

'So, Cathy, shall we have a celebratory drink for a job well done and to our next takedown?'

'I think we should. Wine or fizz?'

'Ooh, a bit of the fizzy stuff is in order.'

'Are you staying over?'

'If that's okay with you.'

'Not a problem you know that Steph.'

'Maybe we should look at the Williams case too?' Said Steph as I popped the cork.

'Nothing in it Steph. After you mentioned it, I did a bit of spiritual detective work. There is nothing amiss as far as I can tell. Best to focus on this Salter scum. We know we have a case with him.'

'Fair enough. I guess if you say there's nothing to dig up, then there's nothing to dig up.'

'You know it— Cheers.'

'Cheers.'

Chapter 26
And Then it all Came Home to Roost

It was a week or so after my celebratory drink with Steph. She stayed over, but no funny business. That was the deal. It was nice to cuddle and be close to one of the last people on earth who I trusted and who I loved so very much. A kindred spirit who was now part of me.

My doorbell rang. As usual, as I was not expecting a visitor, I chained the door before opening it. A man looked at the cracked open door and showed me his ID. Another Police Officer. Reminiscent of my first meeting with good old Brian.

'I'm DCI Salter. I assume you are Catherine Heely?' He said.

The DCI Salter. What was his business here?

'How can I help you?' I asked through the gap.

'Can I come in, please?'

'Not unless you tell me what it's regarding.' *Did that make me seem guilty or just aware of my rights?*

'It's about your former fiancé Paul Jones,' he replied.

'What about him?' I asked dismissively.

'He's dead Ms Heely.'

'What?'

'Look I don't want to discuss this through a crack in the door. Please let me in, or we can do this at the station.'

'Fine come in then.'

I opened the door. Locking it behind us.

'Can I sit.'

'If you must. What does this have to do with me?'

'Well, I thought you might want to know what happened. I thought you'd be at least a little upset.'

'I might have been if he hadn't slept with my sister. I haven't seen or heard from him since we split.'

'Fair enough—I suppose— so you're still angry with him.'

'No—I've simply blocked the whole sorry thing from my mind. So, what happened to him?'

'He was murdered in his apartment. No sign of forced entry. Seemingly nothing was stolen. That would suggest it was personal and someone that he knew. I did speak to your sister Linda, and she said something very interesting.'

'I can't even begin to imagine.'

'Her exact words were; Oh, Cathy's finally lost it then.'

'What does she mean by that? Lost what?'

'I think it's clear what she meant.'

'So, she thinks I killed him so now you do too, that's ridiculous!'

'Well, you would be a potential suspect other than I doubt you have the strength to completely crush his neck. To be honest, it would need a male of incredible size and strength to do it.'

'Oh— that sounds awful. So, if I'm not a suspect, why are you here?'

'The usual questions— did he have enemies Blah blah blah.'

'What do you mean blah blah blah? I don't think anyone hated him that much. He was a nice guy.'

'Well, apart from his infidelities.'

'Well, obviously. But you knew what I meant.'

'Cathy, the plot thickens. In fact, although I haven't quite made the connection. I smell a rat.'

'In what respect do you smell a rat, DCI Salter?'

'Well, you must have seen the news about the Williams kidnapping—'

'Yes— who hasn't.'

'Quite— well when we searched your fiancé's apartment and studio, we found ariel footage of the home of young Kerry Williams and her very wealthy family.'

'Yeah, so Paul did a lot of corporate ariel photography.'

'I know he did. The problem is that when we searched DCI Lyons home. We found lots of obscure occult type reference material and a quite extensive little file on someone he was looking into— off-book or so it seemed. His own little project—any idea who that might have been?'

This was not heading in a direction that I was comfortable with. This bent piece of shit had on the face of it; joined up many dots. How much more did he know? What was his end game? I figured I admit nothing. Let's see how close he was to the truth.

'What is it with all the guessing games? Why would I know who some bent copper was looking into? Maybe he was a stalker as well.'

'Well, he had a comprehensive file on you, Cathy. Statements and recordings of interviews he had done with—well with too many to count. One of them, though, was Paul. And quite recently too.'

'Why would he have a file on me for god's sake?'

'Well given his detailed and thoroughly documented theory. Which is, to say the least, comprehensive and damming. He seemed to think for some reason that you are some sort of witch.'

'Sorry.'

'I have the file right here. There is so much of it.'

Salter produced what was effectively a scrapbook from his briefcase. He flicked through the pages purely for effect.

'look at the list of people in here Cathy. Thomas-blinded. Michael-penectomy-suicide— your dad-stroke – death— Paul-castration- needs updating to say death! — dear Linda-paralysis— mum-fatal heart attack. You seem to be jinxed, Cathy. People around you are dropping like flies.'

'I'm sorry—you need to clarify that. You are here because some corrupt copper who kidnapped a little girl. Had it in his head that I am a witch. Is it me or has the world gone mad? Is it any wonder serious crime goes undetected; when clowns like you are wasting your time investigating witchcraft? It's like Groundhog Day.'

'Yes, it must be. As you had this exact discussion with our Brian just a couple of weeks ago—That's right, isn't it? — says it right here.'

'Just because it says that in the file doesn't make it so. After all, Lyons was clearly a couple of sandwiches short of a picnic!'

'He also claims in here that you slept together— he is extremely complimentary regarding your abilities between the sheets Cathy!'

'So, you fancy your chances too do you? Is that why you're here? —sorry but you're not my type.'

'I might fancy my chances based on what he says in his notes.'

'Like I said, you are taking the word of a madman.'

'I thought you might say something like that. But we also searched the Williams house, and it turns out that Valerie Williams was herself a self-professed witch. Head of the local coven it would seem. I can't believe how many witches are walking amongst us; or so it seems at least. Anyway, Val our High Priestess— had tonnes of witchy paraphernalia to support the fact. Including the extremely rare and very expensive ceremonial knife with which she was slane — somewhat ironically, I might add,' replied Salter, in a very self-assured manner.

'Surely it's all coincidental and circumstantial at best. Paul was legitimately working for Todd's family business. DCI Lyons was fixated on me for some reason.'

'Who mentioned the name, Todd.'

'You did.'

'I Don't think I did.'

'Must have been on the news then.'

'Of course—it must have been.'

'Brian was obsessed with you— but why? How did you know him?'

'Yes, he investigated a case where a boy who tried to rape me then killed himself in front of me.'

'Yes, of course— poor Michael— so, if I was to get a warrant to search your home. Would I find anything that might suggest you are a witch?'

'Yes, you would. My mother was a well-known Medium— Lyons knew that. My mum died recently, but you already know that too. She left me all of her books on the subject. Is that a crime?'

'Lyons notes said you were smart.'

'Well, he got one thing right at least.'

'He said you were cocky too.'

'I was in my mid-teens at the time— what the fuck did he expect. You wouldn't need to be much of a detective to suss that one. Not that he was much of a detective.'

'And sarcastic too. He had you pegged— didn't he?'

'Make of it what you will.'

'Well, there is more Cathy.'

'And what would that be.'

'Well, I have had you watched since I was put on the two cases. It seems that you have ties to a Stephanie Turner. The journalist. The one who cracked the Graham Wainwright murder and exposed a huge drug import business at the same time.'

'Yes, Steph is a good friend. Again, is that a crime?'

'When you opened the door, Cathy. When I showed you my ID. Even through the gap in the door. I could tell that you knew who I was. So, what do you know?' Asked Salter, in quite a sinister tone.

Right— my options were many. Few would end well for this man. I had no protection from the Darkness though, and if Salter jumped me, he might very well overpower me before I could act. I could remove the warding to allow the Darkness to intervene but that required more than a whispered spell. I did have my power-up courtesy of Val and her extraordinary blade. I didn't, however, know what that meant to me in real terms; nor the enhancement that the Darkness had gifted to me.

'I think you are mistaken, officer Salter. I know Steph. But what makes you think that I should know you as a result of knowing her?'

He paused. He was torn. Could he believe the rambling notes of an apparent madman? Was the link between Paul, Todd and Brian connected or merely a coincidence? More importantly, did he believe that I knew he was corrupt. He must know that Steph suspected it. Was she now in danger?

'What was Stephanie's business here?'

'It has nothing to do with you— with all due respect,' I snapped.

'Touchy— is she your girlfriend?'

'It has fuck all to do with you what she is to me.'

'Maybe I need to speak to Todd. I should pay Stephanie a visit too. Oh, Graham's wife. Maybe Graham told her what he knew. What he'd seen. She might be in danger. Be a shame if her and that little boy got shot in the street.'

Salter was now making thinly veiled and obvious threats. He was trying to intimidate me. It was working. I was genuinely scared for my life and the life of my friend; not to mention Grahams wife and son. This man would do what he needed to—he wasn't going to jail that much seemed clear.

'I'm sorry maybe I have missed something. What is it that you think you want from me?'

'If I'm honest, I think I have all I need. You know who I am. Your friend Steph knows who I am. Your eyes gave you away. As soon as you answered the door. I knew. DCI Lyons had said in his notes that your eyes were what gave you away.'

'Yeah and look what happened to him. He was right. But not in the way that you think.'

'So, you do know who I am Cathy?'

'You are a corrupt cop; who was part of the drug import business that Steph brought down. Your mate Eddie will roll over on you in the end.'

'My mate Eddie will be dead by the end of the week.'

Salter smiled. He still hadn't pieced it together though.

'What happens now?' I asked. I needed to know. *I couldn't kill someone without just cause. Not without giving myself to the Darkness.*

'Well, after I've killed you. I will Kill your mate Steph and Graham's wife. Just to be sure we have no loose ends. I will let the boy live though. I'm not completely heartless.'

'How will you do it?'

'Well, I will probably just strangle you— be a shame— you are fucking hot— especially for a witch, in fact, based on Brian's notes, I might have a little ride myself.'

'Yeah— well, we don't all have pointy noses warts and a black hat— Sorry, but this ride is currently closed.'

'You don't seem too flustered Cathy.'

'No— I tend not to get flustered— I kept my cool when I gutted Val Williams with her ceremonial knife, took her soul and then watched her bleed out. I Barely flinched when Todd blew Brian's head off. And only shed a crocodile tear when I crushed Paul's neck; bursting the blood vessels in his eyes as I did it.'

Salter laughed. A little nervously. But he wasn't too phased.

'Nice try Cathy. I don't scare that easy. You don't look like you have it in you if I'm honest. Fact is you are fucked.'

'So, you still haven't put the final piece in the jigsaw, have you?'

'What piece would that be?'

'That I am a witch. An incredibly powerful one. And that you are the one who is going to be getting fucked.'

'This I have to see,' said Salter, as he rose from the chair.

'Just how would you like to die today, officer?' I replied as I too stood.

'What are my options?' He asked with a dismissive smirk.

'In the absence of my bodyguard, I am ever so slightly restricted.'

'So, you have an accomplice, do you? I thought you must have. Is he the one who crushed your boyfriends' neck?'

'Yes— bravo officer— You remember Lyons said that my eyes give me away.'

'He did, yes.'

'Well, tell me what it is that you see now?'

Salter looked at my eyes as I let him see my very own Darkness. The very bottom of my own, incredibly dark soul. This was me— and me alone— this was my rage and my anger— this was my wrath in all of its magnificent glory. At a level of intensity, I'd never felt before. The sensation building throughout my entire body. I felt as though I was about to go super-nova. Salter saw it too. His fate assured. In that split second, he knew it.

I wanted to go all Hollywood on Salter. Explode him. Bleed him slowly from his eyes. Vaporise him. At the same time, I would need to explain his death in my home; as I would be unable to readily remove his body.

What happened next— I didn't even know was within my powers. It just happened. I snatched his soul. I tore it from his chest with my right hand.

I held it in my hands. This ball of energy. He looked at me. I was just as surprised as he was.

The look on Salters face then changed to shock, surprise and then a look of bereavement a look of significant and irreplaceable loss. His arms reached out in an attempt to take it back. His eyes pleading for its return. I felt his overwhelming sadness and crushing sorrow. It was immense. It was almost overwhelming.

For a moment, I forgot my rage and my anger. For a moment, I wanted to hand it back to him.

But then I remembered his threats. I smiled at him as I let it go. It disappeared without a trace. Salter fell back into the chair. He was now completely catatonic.

I called an ambulance, and he was taken to A&E.

Later the police arrived to ask why he was at my home, as he had not logged his visit.

I explained that he had come to threaten me and my friend Steph. That he knew we were aware of his involvement with the recent events. As we had argued, he had suddenly gone vacant and collapsed. That was all I could tell them. I handed them his briefcase—minus, of course, Lyons' scrapbook. *I would burn that later.*

The police called back a week later for a further statement. They told me Salter had been diagnosed with Total Locked-in Syndrome an irreversible condition. The cause was unknown. But it can apparently be caused by nerve damage or damage to the myelin sheath. *So that's what having your soul ripped from your body does to you.*

I was aware that I was beginning to generate a trail of dead and afflicted bodies in my wake. Several people had now connected the dots. I needed to lay low.

Steph called in unannounced the day after my second visit from the police.

'My god Cathy. Why didn't you call me? I just heard from my contact in the Met. Telling me no need to investigate DCI Salter as he is completely catatonic. And that it happened here.'

'It did. I did it to him, Steph.'

'What?'

'He knew that you knew he was corrupt and that I knew too. He was going to kill me and then kill you. So, I stopped him.'

'Are you serious?'

'Yes. Very— '

'How did you do that?'

'I tore his soul out.'

'You did what?'

'Steph— I don't even know how. I just pulled it from his body. He is alive but without a soul.'

'Cathy— my god— what the fuck? —'

'I'm still in shock myself Steph—I will never forget the look on his face.'

'Well—you did what you had to do.'

'I didn't have to do that— I didn't even know that I could. I was so incensed by what he'd said. The next thing I know is that I'm holding his soul in my hand; like a tennis ball.'

'Let's look at the positives, Cathy— you didn't kill anyone.'

'No, Steph— this is worse than that. Much worse.'

'I don't know what else to say, Cathy— except thank you for saving my life. If you had not stopped him, you'd be dead as would I.'

'I think I need to lay low for a while Steph. We can still see each other. In fact, I really want that. But I can't, for now, work any more cases. I hope you understand?'

'Of course I do Cathy. Whatever you want. You can't get rid of me that easy.'

'You are a part of my life Steph and I a part of you. That will never change.'

Chapter 27
Loose Ends

Recent events had made me realise just how vulnerable I potentially was. If the likes of Lyon's and Salter could piece, it together; then so could others.

Steph knew my secrets. She didn't know about my involvement with the Williams kidnap. I didn't want her to know, and I hoped with all that I was; that she would not start poking around in the case.

I did though have two very distinct loose ends. Certainly, loose cannons.

Todd. He could have a change of heart. Develop a guilty conscience. Would he though? He knew the likely consequences if he did. But guilt is a powerful emotion. He might. The bigger question is, would anyone believe him if he suddenly started blaming witches or the devil?

Then I had the loose cannon that was Linda. The sister who hated me before I was even born.

She had maybe pieced things together. She had no proof, but she had a long list of apparent coincidental tragedies that do look increasingly suspicious. She is clearly happy to blab these to anyone who might ask or who is willing to listen; with the full knowledge that in doing so, it creates trouble for me.

With regards to the Linda situation, I had three clear options as I saw it— which though, would win the day— that would depend on Linda!

I decided I would venture out; though I didn't like leaving the house. I needed to do this. I was troubled by the recent events. I would call to see Linda and once and for all, put this to bed.

Linda's children would be at school, and Martin had left her. Not because he was seeing someone else. But ironically because she had slept with Paul. I think the whole disability issue also helped with his decision.

I pressed her intercom to announce my arrival.

'What the hell do you want?' she asked. *What a wonderful greeting.*

'I want to talk Linda.'

'Come to apologise, have you.' *What the hell do I have to apologise for?*

'Something like that.'

She buzzed the door open.

'I'm in the lounge,' she shouted as I closed the door.

'Hi Linda, — how are you?'

'How do you think I am?'

'Look, let's not start with an argument. I need to chat with you. I have a huge decision ahead of me, and I need to know where we stand before I make it.'

'Listen if you want a drink help yourself— I'll have tea milk no sugar if you wouldn't mind.'

'Yeah— sure.'

I dutifully made our drinks and returned to the lounge.

Linda was in her wheelchair. A lovely state of the art electrically powered model.

'So, sis— to what do I owe this extremely rare and unannounced visit?' asked Linda.

'I want to talk about us—you and me— how we ended up like this. We are sisters we should be close we should have each other's backs— not be sticking knives in them.'

'That's aimed at me; I take it?'

'Look stop— we won't get anywhere if all you do is play the victim.'

'I am the victim—I'm in a fucking wheelchair for god's sake. My husband abandoned me. My children hate me.'

'Have you asked yourself why that might be?'

'Because of you. You caused all of this. I know you did.'

'And what is that supposed to mean?'

'Cathy— I know.'

'Know what?'

'You're a witch just like mum was— only more powerful.'

'Why do you think that?'

'Cathy— you came here for a chat at least do me the courtesy of being honest. You owe me that. Stop with the bullshit—'

'So, I have some powers— why does that have to make you hate me so?'

'Okay— I was jealous at first. A new baby. You are getting all the attention. Me feeling left out.'

'Those are perfectly normal feelings to have. But they continued and grew into a hatred of me. Yet I never did anything to fuel that— so why?'

'Because I was jealous of you. But that turned to fear after you made me sick. I saw it in your eyes even as a three-year-old, I knew what that was.'

'Linda—I am so sorry. I didn't do that to you the Darkness did it.'

'Yeah— I heard you and mum mention this Darkness. Seems a convenient excuse if you ask me—You are just evil sis.'

'I may well be—, but I never wanted to harm you.'
'Yet here I am.'
'You think I did this to you?'
'I know you did.'

I wanted to clear the air. That is why I had come here. Linda knew or suspected me of striking her down. Is this an amnesty or a confessional? My eyes got a little teary.

'I did do this to you, Linda. I caught you in bed with Paul. When I act in rage and anger, I have less control over the punishment I administer. But the Darkness wanted me to kill you. I chose not to.'

'I wish you had. I hate this life— if you can even call it that.'

'Why didn't you say something before now? I was wracked with guilt for what I had done to you both.'

'What difference would it have made?'

'So why did you tip off the police. Saying they should look into mum's death?'

'What?'

Yeah— that DCI Lyons the one you spilt your guts to. He said they had received an anonymous tip from a woman.'

'Sorry! I did know DCI Lyons—but it didn't come from me, I swear.'

'He tried to kill me, him, Paul and those Williams fuckers from the news.'

'What the fuck?'

'I Know.'

'I had a DCI Salter come to interview me about Paul.'

'Yes, he said he'd be calling to see you.'

'You killed them all, didn't you, Cathy?'

Wow straight to the point there sis. Do I come clean? Eeny, meeny, miny, moe— fuck it.

'Okay— Yes— but it was all in self-defence.'

'What about mum?'

'It's complicated Linda. The alternatives were unthinkable— I'm sorry. I really am.'

'Death seems to be the norm for you. The number of people you have killed or struck down over the years is staggering. You seem so calm and matter of fact about it. You killed mum you killed dad after first making him suffer. But you barely shed a tear.'

'I have cried Linda. Believe me, I have cried. I am cursed. I am tormented constantly by the Darkness. It is real. I don't want to hurt people. But they seem to want to hurt me. I just want to live my solitary life without having the likes of Lyons and Salter beating on my door. You need to stop trying to stitch me up. Please.'

'Or else you will kill me too?'

'Why would you even say that Linda?'

'That's why you are here. Sound me out. Get me on-side. Or silence me for good?'

'I just want you to stop this vendetta you have. I tried to love you, Linda. You made that impossible. Not Me.'

'You'd might as well kill me. You did mum and dad. Make it a full-house a hat-trick.'

'I am not here to kill you, Linda. I don't have much in my life that I care about. I want to try and make this work between us.'

'Then undo what you did to me.'

'I would if I could, Linda.'

'You haven't even tried.'

'I don't have the powers to reverse what I do.'

'You brought a dead bird back to life— but you can't fix my legs?'

'I can fix and cure things, not of my own doing. I cannot reverse the things that I have done.'

'How do you know if you don't try.'

'I tried with dad— believe me, I tried.'

'You are older now— maybe your powers are stronger.'

'I can try if it would make you feel better. But I'm pretty sure it won't work.'

I wrestled Linda onto the couch. Facedown. I placed my hands at the base of her spine, and for all I was worth I tried to sense the damaged nerves and repair them. I channelled all I had into undoing what I had done.

'I can feel sensation in my legs Cathy. It's working. Don't stop.'

I continued until I felt physically and emotionally exhausted. I turned her and sat her upright on the couch. At which point I was totally spent.

'Well?' I asked.

Linda studied for a moment. Then she looked down at her feet.

'Oh my god, Cathy— I can move my toes— you did it.'

I too looked at her feet. Her toes were indeed moving.

'Wow. Okay— let's not get carried away it will take you weeks even months to rebuild your wasted muscle. You will need specialist physiotherapy. Do not try and rush things.'

'Cathy— Thank you. You have no idea what this means to me. You have given me back my life.'

'My powers must still be increasing— that's not supposed to happen.'

'Well— let's not look a gift horse in the mouth Cathy.'
'Can we start over Linda?'
'Cathy, all we have now is each other.'
'Well— you do have your two children as well, Linda.'
'I told you they hate me.'
'But that's because you were angry with life. Angry at me. Give it another chance. You owe that to them. But more importantly, Linda, you owe it to yourself.'
'No—I will let Martin have custody—it's just you and me against the world sis.'
'Linda— you need to cherish your children. I want us to be friends. But I choose to live a solitary life. We won't be out every night on the pull together. We won't be having road trips or holidays in the sun. We will just be two sisters who are good friends.'
'So, I am still not good enough for you? Is that it?'
'Don't be silly, Linda. I just think you need to enjoy the lovely family you have. Shake off all the anger, resentment and bitterness that has held you back all these years. Enjoy life— I can't enjoy life, but you can.'
'Listen, you have given me back what you took from me. That does not mean you have the right to tell me how to live my life.'
'What you and Paul did Linda. Took more from me than you will ever know. Take this chance I've given you.'
'Fuck you, Cathy. I'll do what I want with my life. You have no say what I do. Who I speak to? Or who I tell about my dear little sister the witch.'
'I can take it all back, Linda.'
'You wouldn't dare.'
'Try me.'

'You strike me down again. I will shout it from the highest hills.'

'Let me tell you something, Linda. The decision I needed to make was whether I should silence you permanently. I'd hoped our little chat would satisfy me that it would not be necessary. Look at you. Ungrateful bitch. I give you yet another chance. Another chance to be a decent human being. Are you really so irreparably damaged from your jealousy and hatred of me?'

'If you kill me; you will have murdered your entire family. Can you live with that on your conscience— do you even have a conscience?'

'You do what you need to do, Linda. I will have no further hand in your fate. I hope you see sense before it really is too late. If you change your mind, you know where to find me. Goodbye, Linda.'

I felt a mixture of emotions as I made a coffee and sat in my armchair. Back safely in my warded castle. Giving Linda back the use of her legs had lifted the burden of guilt I carry. I was also saddened that even now Linda hated me still. If she decided to blab to the authorities, I would take the fallout as it comes. I had done all I could to find the good in Linda. I could do no more. I would not strike her down. Not again.

Chapter 28
Here We Go Again

It had been some two years since I'd last spoken to Linda. I assumed as there were no knocks on my door that she had considered her position and seen sense finally. She had never however, contacted me.

My friendship with Steph continued much as before. My friend Jenny kept in touch, and we saw each other at least monthly.

I never did tell Jenny about my curse. As I became more reclusive, the closeness of our relationship had diminished some. I still loved her to bits. But we didn't get out together. Jenny continued with her art and was a sought-after designer of tattoo art as well as a children's book illustrator. Jenny was also in a medium-term relationship, so our relationship was now purely platonic. Jenny would continue to try and coax me out of the house. I did occasionally venture out but never felt entirely at ease.

I was scrying a little more often. My communication with Madimi was beneficial in maintaining my sanity.

We had discussed the blade of Nalvage. It may have been in police evidence, but due to its monetary value, I assumed that the Williams family would request it be returned.

This blade held far more than monetary value though, and Madimi told me that I should attempt to retrieve it.

I was unsure about how I would even begin to do so. But as luck might have it, the problem would solve itself. When I say luck. I didn't necessarily mean good luck.

It was mid-December; early evening. My phone rang. It Was Jenny.

'Hi there Jen—'

'Cathy—' Replied Jenny, sounding somewhat upset and distressed.

'Jen— What's wrong— are you okay?'

'She is fine— whether she stays that way is up to you, Cathy,' replied the man who had now taken over the conversation. His voice seemed familiar, but it didn't register— not yet at least.

'Who is this? And what are you doing with Jenny?'

'I'm disappointed you don't remember me. As you slaughtered my sister in front of me.'

'Todd— I thought we had an agreement?'

'Did you think that having watched you disembowel my sister in front of me that I could let it go? You were always going to have to pay Cathy.'

'I let you live Todd. I could have killed you. But I let you live.'

'Well let that be a lesson, Cathy.'

'So, what do you want?'

'I want you to come to me so that I can kill you. If you don't, I will kill Jenny.'

'Maybe I call the police, and they come to your home and arrest you.'

'I'm not home, and you won't know where I am until you get here.'

'And how's that?'

'A Car will pick you up in five minutes. If you fail to get in; Jenny dies.'

'Okay if this is how you want to do it, Todd.'

'It is Cathy— the driver will drop you off; and then I will call you to guide you the last few hundred metres.'

'Fine then.'

'I look forward to seeing you again, Cathy.'

As I hung up the phone, I heard the toot of the horn from henchmen taxi services. I grabbed my jacket, slipped on my trainers and headed out of the door.'

As I sat in the back of the car, I wondered just what I was walking into. My options were not quite as peachy as my last encounter with Todd; as I could not be possessed by the Darkness for a second time. He would be there, but that may not be enough. They would likely have warding again and be unlikely to repeat their previous errors. It was also very likely that Todd would have assistance so I would be physically outgunned. Todd was not the smartest, but he'd had two years to plot his revenge. Maybe my time was up.

The Taxi ride was about half an hour. As I alighted the vehicle, my phone rang.

'Cathy, you see the Church across the way. The one with the scaffolding. Knock at the door.'

The phone went dead before I could respond.

I knocked as instructed at the door to the church. Clearly one of Todd's dad's developments. A church being converted to apartments. The door was opened by one of Todd's burly looking henchmen. He invited me in and pointed me to a seat.

'Please sit-down Cathy,' said Todd, 'if you try anything, Jenny will die.'

Jenny was sat in a similar chair to mine; her hands tied to the arms of the chair; her legs bound to the legs of the chair. She had clearly been crying but did not look injured. Another of Todd's henchmen was stood with the blade of Nalvage at Jenny's throat. It was Todd plus two. Two thugs that looked as though they would relish killing us both.

'Why are you doing this Todd? We had a deal. Jenny is not part of this, so let her go.'

'We have been chatting Jenny and me. You two are very close. I know that is rare for you, Cathy. You seem to have two friends in the whole world. Jenny here and some journalist called Stephanie. You see I have been watching you. Looking to find your weakness. To find something you might love as much as I had loved my sister.'

'Your sister was prepared to kill you and her own daughter; I fail to see why you feel you owe her anything.'

'She was my sister, my blood, and you slaughtered her.'

'It was self-defence, and you know it.'

'No, you toyed with us, like a cat toys with a mouse. You enjoyed it.'

'I do not enjoy killing Todd. I did what I had to do.'

'Well, it seems you neglected to tell your special friend Jenny here. That you are a witch.'

I looked at Jenny's face. Her panda eyes from her mascara mixed with her tears. To say she looked confused would be an understatement.

'Cathy is it true? — you've killed people?' sobbed Jenny.

'Jenny— it's not how they make it sound.'

'Have you killed people?'

'Yes, I have.'

'Are you really a witch like they say you are?'

'I am a witch of sorts Jenny— it's a little more complicated than that though.'

'I thought we were friends— why couldn't you tell me?'

'For exactly this reason, Jenny. Anyone who knows my secret seems to come unstuck. I didn't want you getting hurt because of me. I love you. I could not bear to see you get hurt.'

'Well isn't this nice. A little heart to heart. I'm getting all misty-eyed,' sneered Todd.

'Todd please reconsider what you are doing. I saw good in you. This doesn't have to go down like this.'

'Cathy, you are going to watch me gut your friend. As I watched you gut my sister. I even have the knife you used. Then I am going to gut you and get your power-up.'

'Todd you said Jenny would not be hurt if I came to you. And the knife only does that if you strike down evil, I'm not evil.'

'Yeah, you told my sister you would spare her if she killed me. But you lied. And I think you are evil, Cathy. You are just in denial about it.'

'Do what you want to me. But please, I beg you— Jenny has nothing to do with this. Your sister was a willing participant. Jenny is not.'

'That's just too bad Cathy. Now my two associates want to get to know Jenny a little better. She is pretty. You can watch them have a bit of fun. As you know. Ever since I first met you. I wanted you! So Jenny can watch while you and I get better acquainted then you can both die. How does that sound?'

'It sounds sick, Todd. So why did you pick the church? Did you think it would offer you protection from my powers?'

'No, I just thought it would be both cool and sick at the same time. Of course, it protects us. It is hallowed ground your friend the Darkness cannot operate here and you my dear are in the equivalent of safe mode. You will end up in the concrete floors, so you can haunt the place for all eternity.'

'You seem to have done your homework Todd is that why you haven't bound me?'

'Yes, my sister made a simple error. I won't be caught out. You, Cathy, are fucked.

'Todd, I gave you the chance to do the right thing, and you took it. Do the same now, and I won't be forced to kill the three of you.'

'Cathy, your poker-faced bluffs won't work this time. Now get ready for a hot sex show. Do you think Jenny likes anal? I guess we'll find out won't we.'

'Todd wait— let me say one more thing before we get started.'

'What now, Cathy. You're out of chips. I called— you folded.'

'Hear me out.'

'These will be some of your final words, so make them count.'

Jenny was looking at me. Fear in her eyes. The two henchmen were stood either side of her. She knew what they intended to do. I could not— I would not let them hurt her.

'In order to make this church into apartments Todd, you would need to get the church or the diocese to lift the covenant that existed here.'

'Yes, but a covenant is just an agreement contained in the deeds that prevents a change of use.'

'Yes, it is— but when the church lifts its covenant, it also lifts the religious covenant which is completely different. It means that unless the church has a graveyard. Which this one does not. That the churches sacred ground status is also withdrawn. This church now offers no more protection than did your sisters warding on her home.'

'You never let up, do you? But you were possessed by the Darkness last time, and you can't do that again. So nice try.'

'You are correct, Todd, you have done your homework.'

'Yes, I have spoken in depth with some of the other witches from my sister's coven.'

'Ah— more amateurs, you see I received a power-up from your whore of a sister as well as a Brucey bonus from the Darkness. So, I can fuck you all up regardless. Last chance to back down boys.'

It was a little like Groundhog Day. Todd looked to see if he could spot a tell. He couldn't. He clearly remembered what had happened last time, and knew, there was no escape for him if I was telling the truth. The knife was now back at Jenny's throat as the tension started to rise.

'You know that if you strike down an innocent with the blade of Nalvage, it is like a gun backfiring. It will kill the holder of the blade. They do not get any more innocent than Jenny, so you might want to be careful with that.'

'Yes, but Jenny still dies.'

'Yes, she does, but so will your poor henchman. I'm not sure he signed up for that. Did you, pal?' I replied as I looked over to Jenny's knife-wielding henchman.

'Bullshit,' replied Todd.

'Well kill her then. Did you tell your two hired guns the whole story, Todd? Or did you leave out the best bits?'

By now, the man holding the knife was clearly having second thoughts. Suddenly loyalties became questionable.

'He didn't tell you how it went down with his sister, did he? —you wouldn't be here if he had,' I asked the two men.

'Don't fucking listen to her; she is all talk boys.'

'Did Todd tell you how I gutted his sister? — I lifted her with one hand using that very knife— I spilled her guts all over the floor of her study— he didn't tell you that did he? — Did you Todd?'

'She is bull-shitting you— don't listen to her.'

'Are you paying these boys enough to die for you Todd? To die for your fucked-up idea of revenge?'

'Strip the bitch, bend her over that bench and get fucking her,' ordered Todd.

'Don't do it boys— it will be the last thing that you ever do I promise.'

Beads of sweat were now visible on both the henchmen's foreheads.

'For fuck's sake. Give me the fucking knife will you?' demanded Todd.

It seemed clear now that Todd's two rent-a-thugs were having more than second thoughts; they were ready to leave. It looked like I might bluff my way out of this, after all.

'Todd you're on your own now. Just walk away. Live to fight another day.'

'You fucking bitch.'

'Nobody need die today Todd. Is that really such a bad thing?'

Todd looked defeated.

'Untie her,' I instructed the knife-wielding henchman.

He began to untie Jenny.

'We are leaving now Todd. Be glad you made the right choice.'

'We are not done, witch.'

'You know where to find me, Todd.'

Jenny and I were almost at the door when I paused.

'Jenny wait here a moment. I will only be a minute I forgot something.'

Poor Jenny was trembling from the fright. I needed the blade and the door key.

'What the fuck are you doing now?' asked Todd.

'I need the door key, and I need the blade too, Todd— give it to me.'

'No chance— you really are pushing your luck.'

'Just hand it over, Todd. It is of no use to you.'

'And what is your interest in it?'

'To keep it safe— nothing more.'

'Sorry— it's not happening.'

'I will take it from you if I have to.'

Todd signalled to the two reluctant henchmen to protect him, which they dutifully did.

'So, you are back in the game boys?' I said with a smile.

'I have changed my mind, Cathy— I think you are bluffing. I will let your friend watch us fuck you so hard you'll beg to die.'

'Why is it that everyone always wants to fuck me first. Is it a dominance thing? Does it make you feel that you have power over me? I know I'm hot, but I'm tired of hearing the same old shit— I told you before Todd I am out of your league.'

'We're going to work you real good Cathy—'

'Todd, you and your boys, couldn't even get me warmed up; no matter how hard and long you fucked me.'

'I guess we'll see about that,' said Todd, as the two henchmen grabbed my arms.

I really did want to see if I could end this without anyone having to die. That's a lie actually— they were all dead the moment they called me. I just wanted to test my self-control. I'd hoped that my poker face had convinced them to walk away. Or at least believe they could walk away. — *Why do men have to be so fucking stupid?*

I had been in an Enochian conversation with the Darkness the whole time. We had looked at the various options for smiting these sorry individuals. As usual, the Darkness wanted me to crush them without mercy or compassion. I knew he had been right. I should not have spared Todd in the first place. Will I ever learn? I had not wanted to finish this with Jenny present. I had not wanted Jenny to see that side of me that would momentarily manifest itself. This time my wrath would be bloody, it would be biblical. My friend had been threatened. She would likely never get over the incident. What I was about to do would add to her distress. For that, I was sorry. But I now had no choice as the two-henchman pulled me to the rape rack they had previously prepared for Jenny and me. Todd followed with the blade and a perverse look on his face.

Unlike my previous encounter with Todd, I was not immortal, and I did not have the strength of ten men. However, my power-up from Todd's sister Val did mean I was as strong as two men.

As I was dragged backwards onto the bench, Todd approached. I deliberately began to open my legs.

'No need to be rough boys— I'm going to fuck your brains out,' I said as Todd approached me.

The blade was curved a little like a scythe. It had a sharp edge. But in the right hands, it had an edge so fine and sharp it could not be seen by the naked eye. It will slice through bone like butter.

Todd placed the hooked end of the knife in my knickers to cut them from me; as he did, I threw off the grip of the two henchmen and sat up; grabbing the blade from Todd in one continuous movement.

I held the knife— hooked end pointing up and before Todd could even think the blade entered that sweet spot. The perineum. Todd looked down as he felt the blade enter him. He then looked at my face. With all my might, I drew the knife upward. Cutting his scrotum open as his testicles fell to the floor, their blood vessels and vas deferens severed. His penis was sliced neatly in half down its length as the blade continued its upward travel. His intestines burst from his abdomen and fell to the floor along with his liver and kidneys. The blade finished its travel in his sternum. I withdrew the blade from him. He fell to the floor, almost sliced in two; looking like a slaughtered pig at the abattoir; Todd's heart still beating his eyes open; he looked at me as I stood over him; drenched in his blood and a look of crazed satisfaction on my face. The last thing he would ever know. His soul no more.

The two henchmen had by now grabbed poor Jenny, and one was holding a box cutter knife to her throat.

'Boys— I said I would let you go. If you hurt my friend, I will show you no quarter. Let her go, and we can sort this out like grownups. If you hurt her I will make you eat each other's balls before killing you.'

I had, of course, received another power-up from the killing of Todd. The power felt all-consuming. It felt almost as it had when I had been possessed by the Darkness.

'Let her go now— you have until the count of five to let her go— look at Todd— do you want to die like that? Because you will, if you don't let her go right now.'

'I'll slit her throat if you don't back off bitch,' said the man holding the knife.

'Look I don't even know your name—'

'Dan—'

'Look, Dan, how many ways can I say it— if you hurt my friend, I will kill you—do you understand?'

'You'll kill us anyway.'

'I didn't want any of this— we were leaving without bloodshed, but Todd had to spoil it—we can all just walk away from this. Just let Jenny go, Dan. You have my word— I won't harm you.'

Dan processed my offer. He looked at Todd's filleted remains. His gut's, organs and testicles were strewn across the ground. He looked at the blade in my hand. The look in my eyes. He listened so carefully to the tone of my voice. The demonic inflexion of my words. He lowered the knife from Jenny's carotid artery and pushed her towards me.

Jenny continued towards me as I beckoned for her to stand behind me. Dan and his accomplice stood side by side. Looking. Waiting. Wondering.

'Okay Dan that was the right thing to do,' I said as I lowered the blade and walked towards them.

'You made a mistake. You picked the wrong fight. You backed the wrong horse. But it's over now.'

The two breathed a sigh of relief as I reached where they stood. Both looked relieved to have been spared.

'What now?' asked Dan as he looked over to Todd's body.

'What do you think we should do Dan? — I'm open to suggestions, but I think Todd's past the point of needing urgent medical attention, don't you?'

'We all just leave—' suggested Dan.

'The issue with that Dan— is that I let Todd live the last time we met. How do I know I can trust you to keep quiet about what went on here tonight?'

'I swear we won't say a fucking word.'

'So, Dan— I promised to let you go if you released my friend and I keep my word.'

'Yes, yes, you seem like someone who keeps their word.'

'I am. My word is my bond. The problem I have is that it wasn't me who made that promise. It was the Darkness. He is testing me to see if I have learned my lesson.'

'And have you?'

'Yes Dan, I have.'

'Good—' replied Dan as he smiled in secondary relief. Smiling at his friend as he did.

'Yes, I have learned my lesson well Dan— there can be no loose ends.'

As my words rang out, I swung the blade with all the power I could muster. The shocked look on their faces fixed forever as both their heads hit the floor. A fountain of blood from their decapitated bodies drenched me, as they too fell to the floor. *Fuck that blade is sharp.*

Jenny froze; speechless. Seeing one of her best friends stood over the two bodies. Looking like a victorious gladiator. Drenched in the blood of my enemies.'

I looked at her face as it tried to register what had just happened. She looked at me, she looked at the blade that I still held in my tightly clenched hand.

'No loose ends—' she said with a look of inevitability on her face.

I smiled with an acknowledging smile.

'That's right, Jenny—no loose ends— sorry but they had to die. Come on, let's get out of here. Back to my place, we need a chat.'

'What? — fuck, Cathy, I thought you were going to kill me too.'

'Jenny if I was going to kill you, I wouldn't have bothered coming here in the first place—you muppet.'

'Fuck Cathy— I just pissed my effing pants.'

'Never mind— Come on, let's go.'

'Cathy you can't walk the streets looking as though you just slaughtered the entire population of a small South American country. Let me bring you a change of clothes. I'll be back in half an hour. Use the hosepipe over there, to wash yourself down.'

'You did well, Jenny. Most people would be completely freaked out right now. You seem okay— quite functional, in fact.'

'I am far from okay, Cathy. But once I saw you dispatch Todd; I knew we'd make it through. I am not sure I will ever sleep again, mind. Maybe it's the adrenalin I don't know. But for now, we need to get you a change of clothes. I will be half an hour tops.'

'Okay. Todd has the door key in his pocket— shall I get it?'

'Yeah— if you don't mind.'

'Wimp.'

As Jenny left, I considered the possibilities. Would she come back at all? Would she come back with the police? Was she a loose end like Linda? Like Todd had been! Could I kill her? Should I kill her? Would this torment ever end while ever someone knew the truth about me?

Jenny did return. She arrived with a change of clothes exactly as she said she would. I had cleared the scene of any evidence that Jenny and I had ever been there. Let the police make of it what they will. I painted the walls with devil worship symbols using the blood; of which there was ample. I Made it look like the scene of some devil worship ritual gone wrong. Some of the symbols I used were very rare, unusual and obscure— not the typical fare associated with amateurs who have read a couple of books they bought on Amazon. The fact Val had been a self-proclaimed high priestess should muddy the water enough. *An extreme case of misadventure.*

Two more power-ups. I was now giddy and intoxicated by the sensation. I was primed. I felt as though my very humanity was being devoured from within. I needed to catch my breath before I crossed the point of no return. How much more would I be capable of? Would it be good? Would it be deadly? Could I contain it? Could I control it? Was the Darkness winning me over?

Had the Darkness engineered this whole situation with this purpose in mind?

Chapter 29
The Aftermath

Jenny and I arrived at my place in the early hours. We got a taxi but not to my street. We were dropped two streets away and gave a fake address just in case cab drivers were interviewed about their fares that evening.

We knew our phone GPS would give away our locations, but we would need to be suspects in the first place so that should not be an issue. It is unlikely that the police would be looking for two women given the extent of the injuries inflicted on Todd and his henchmen.

Jenny had the presence of mind to bring the change of clothes in a rucksack which I was then able to stash the knife and bloodied garments in.

As I unlocked the front door, we both stepped in and breathed a huge sigh of relief that we were back on safe ground. I locked the door.

'Right Jenny— I need a drink— crack open the whiskey, will you? I need to light my log burner and destroy these clothes.'

'Okay— do you still take it with a splash of water?'

'I do, yes. Bring the bottle through.'

I threw in some firelighters and a handful of sticks and set the log burner going.

I took a seat while the fire took hold.

'I think you have some explaining to do Cathy— What the hell did I just witness?'

'You witnessed me at my very worst and at my very best.'

'How do you figure— I just watched you kill three grown men like you was swatting flies.'

'What did they tell you?'

'They said you are a witch and that you killed Todd's sister and Paul— something about you causing a police officer to go into a permeant state of catatonia and that you made Todd shoot another police officer— is that true Cathy? Did you really do all that they said you did?'

'Yes— but just as tonight Jen it was in self-defence.'

'How can you even do that? — I mean both mentally and physically?'

'Because I am a powerful witch, and because in simple terms, the devil is effectively my guardian angel.'

Jenny looked at me as though I was some crazy asylum escapee. But she also knew what she had witnessed with her own eyes.

'You work with the devil?'

'No, I don't— I try to do good— my powers are immense—'

'— I'll say.'

'The Darkness, as I call it, wants me to give myself to him.'

'What? — he wants you as some sort of sidekick does he?'

'I guess you could call it that. But if I used my powers for evil Jen, I would lay waste to the earth.'

'You're kidding, right?'

'Nope— killing people with that blade increases my powers significantly both in extent and in magnitude. I dread to think what I am now capable of— excuse me I need to throw some coal on the fire.'

I opened the fire door and put some coal on the kindling that was now well ablaze.

'I'll give it five and then burn the rucksack and its contents.'

'So how long have you been super-witch?'

'Since I was born.'

'Were you ever going to tell me? — my god, the things you did to me when we slept together— that's not because you're just good in bed— that was witchy shit?'

'A bit of both Jen— I wanted to tell you, but it's such a huge burden to bear. It also puts you potentially in harm's way— tonight being a good example— I wanted to protect you Jen, not deceive you.'

'So, this is why you lock yourself away?'

'Yes, I can't be trusted.'

'You are quite simply one of the nicest people I know Cathy.'

'Maybe so— but it's other people. I just get so angry and when I do— well you've just seen what happens.'

'That was self-defence Cathy.'

'So you don't think I should have just incapacitated them and then called the police?'

'You tried to walk away Cathy—'

'No Jen— I didn't— I never intended— not even for a moment to leave that church with any of them still breathing— I had to kill them, or they would have just kept trying until one day they succeeded.'

'You did what you had to do— it was gross but necessary—'

'What? — I needed to slaughter Todd like some pig in an abattoir, to bathe in his blood and watch the life fade from his eyes as I killed his soul— is that not a little excessive in your eyes?'

'I suppose if you put it like that Cathy—'

'Worse still, Jen— I enjoyed it. It was intoxicating— invigorating; I fucking revelled in it.'

'We all have a dark side, Cathy,' said Jen with an awkward smile.

'And that's why I love you, Jen. What is the darkest thing you have ever done— given someone the middle finger when they cut you up at the traffic lights?'

'No— I would never do something so crass,' she laughed.

'I rest my case Jen— there's having a dark side, and then there's having a dark side.'

'So, what do we do if the police come knocking?'

'Just let me throw that rucksack on the fire.'

I again opened the stove door and threw in the rucksack minus the blade of Nalvage and returned to my seat.

'They won't come calling— they cannot place us at the scene.'

'What if they do? What if Todd left a note to say if anything happens to him that the police should question you?'

'I think he was just so arrogant he thought he had it all covered. He never considered a back-up. But he may have done— that's a fair point. It would change things as they would be able to check our phone records. I'm sure Todd wasn't that smart though.'

'I hope you're right— What about that knife? — that's the murder weapon.'

'I will put it somewhere safe.'

'What is that anyway?'

'It's an extraordinary knife created by an angel called Nalvage; he is the slayer of beasts.'

'What's that when it's at home?'

'The blade kills evil— and it also destroys the soul of the victim. So, they don't go to heaven or hell. They cannot ever be redeemed or reborn. They quite simply never existed.'

'Wow— that's a serious bit of kit. What else does it do?'

'It gives the holder of the knife added powers each time they kill evil using it.'

'What like picking up a mushroom in Mario Kart?'

'Yes for want of a better euphemism— it's a permanent power-up— the sensation is hard to describe; it is as though you just want to go on a killing spree— the thing is it would be a killing spree directed at people who are evil. I can see how succumbing to it would be like becoming a drug addict. It is all that you can think about— your next fix— in this case, your next kill. I struggled to stop. It took all that I had not to spill out into the street and slaughter everything in my path that I saw as evil.'

'My god Cathy— can you actually see evil?'

'I have always been able to sense it in people that I touch. But with the blade in my hand, I can see evil clearly. It is almost like them having a huge neon sign over their head saying; I'm evil please kill me.'

'So, you are super-witch. The slayer of evil.'

'I could be— the thing is I think it would ultimately turn me into something else. I could feel it growing in me. If I feed it— it will eventually consume me.'

'You probably need to meditate or something— clear your head.'

'Only my darling Jen could suggest I meditate after just slaughtering three people. That is why I love you so, Jen.'

'I love you too, Cathy.'

'Will you stay Jen. Just cuddles. You have always had a calming effect on me. You settle me. You're like my real-life little comfort blanket.'

'Of course I will stay, Cathy. I need that too after what we've just been through.'

'You still want to be friends then?'

'Well I will never see you quite the same again Cathy— but we've been so close for so long— all I saw was a woman who acted in self-defence to save herself and to save me. How can I hate you for saving my life?'

'I would hate not having you in my life, Jen— you mean the world to me.'

'Come on then I don't know about super-witch, but I for one am knackered.'

Chapter 30
Me. Myself & Madimi

I decided to contact Madimi. I now had the blade of Nalvage, and I needed to know what was happening to my powers and perhaps more importantly, what was happening to me.

I prepared, as I always did and began my session.

'Catherine— I am here. I see you have the blade of Nalvage.'

'Yes, I do, and I have taken three more souls with it.'

'Catherine, you must be careful—the blade is not all that it seems.'

'I might have known— What do you mean by that Madimi?'

'When the blade takes a soul, you receive the pure power; cleansed of the evil it once held. But the blade absorbs that evil. Eventually, the holder of the blade will become overwhelmed by this evil.'

'I did feel that.'

'The last mortal to use the blade was Vlad the third Dracula.'

'Vlad the Impaler?'

'Yes, Catherine— he began his journey simply wanting to win back his country and avenge the death of his father and brother. He became consumed, and he was responsible for tens of thousands of deaths as the blade grew in power, so his bloodlust grew with it.'

'So, where has the knife been since the fifteenth century?'

'It was lost in battle. It was unearthed some ten years ago in Turkey. Nobody knew what it was. But it had the crest of the Basarab dynasty linking it to Dracula, so it sold almost as a novelty item. If you consider a half-million dollars to be a novelty item.'

'And it was Valerie Williams who bought it?'

'Yes.'

'She had no clue what it was; did she?'

'No— or she would almost certainly have used it to enhance her powers.'

'What am I to do Madimi— I want to use my powers for good. But now I have these added powers I have no idea what I am capable of.'

'All of your existing powers are improved— you must already feel that.'

'Yes, I do— but it's the new powers I don't even know about until I use them. That's what worries me— just what am I now able to do Madimi?'

'Many of your powers will only function if you are in danger, or extremely angry and if you are holding the blade. In such cases, you will be incredibly strong—'

'Is that it?'

'No Catherine it is not— you will be able to withstand great pain. Your wounds, unless fatal, will heal quickly.'

'No new magic then?'

'No new magic, Catherine— Do you not have enough already?'

'I have too much Madimi— I just want to be normal— that is all I ever wanted.'

'You must find ways to use your powers for good Catherine. You should not let them go to waste.'

'But I always end up in trouble. Someone always seems to die.'

'You need to think carefully, Catherine. Helping your friend Stephanie is a good example of what you can do.'

'The Darkness is watching me. This is my only sanctuary. These four walls are my protectors and also my prison.'

'You can resist the Darkness, Catherine. You have done so many times over the years.'

'But half the time, the Darkness has been right about things, and I didn't listen. I then ended up in an even worse situation.'

'He wants you to think he is your friend— your protector. In some ways, he is. But it is all in an effort to win your allegiance to him.'

'I know, but if he catches me at the right moment, I fear I will give in to him— sometimes I even fantasise about what it might be like. When the Darkness that is my own takes hold of me, I struggle to come back from it. It frightens me, but at the same time, it excites me. I feel the bloodlust. Even before I had used the blade, I felt it.'

'You always come back Catherine because you are an inherently good person.'

'Yes, people keep telling me what a good person I am— I just slaughtered three defenceless people Madimi— what's so good about that?'

'They weren't defenceless Catherine.'

'But they were against me Madimi. The dice were loaded from the start. I knew it— they didn't.'

'They made a choice Catherine— they would have killed you had they had the chance. They acted upon their own free will, and there were severe consequences for them as a result. But it was their choice. Don't ever forget that, Catherine.'

'And yet I know, I need not have killed them.'

'And yet you did— what would have been gained by letting them live?'

'They would be alive.'

'Life is precious, Catherine— I understand your concerns. But if people choose to abuse the gift of life and that of free will then they should be punished, if not, evil will prevail. You can see it everywhere, Catherine— you know it to be true.'

'What would you suggest I do with the blade Madimi?'

'I would suggest that you use it, Catherine. Not excessively but sparingly. You should use your powers to find and destroy evil.'

'I would quickly be dubbed a serial killer and be on the countries most wanted list. I don't think so Madimi.'

'I understand your reservations, Catherine, but you are incredibly intelligent and insightful; you could make it work— you know you could.'

'No— Okay— NO!'

'Very well then hide the blade in your well in the cellar it won't corrode. There is a ledge about two feet down. Place it there.'

'I will— thank you.'

'I should leave now, Catherine— we will speak again soon. I am sure of it.'

So, the daughter of the angel of light would like me to turn slayer in the name of good. Effectively become some superhero; out there killing evil. It's an intriguing thought. I always secretly fancied myself a superhero. How would that even work? If I get caught even carrying that blade it's straight to jail, do not pass go. Crazy notion. Forget it— NO!

Chapter 31
When I say no—

After the incident with Todd and Jenny; and my subsequent conversations with Madimi, I spent several months taking stock of my situation.

Thankfully I received no visits from the police. The incident had made the national news as might well be expected. The father of Todd; Philip Clarke, in an interview; said that he would use his substantial wealth to bring to justice those responsible for the death of his son, he also indicated that he believed his sister's murder was also linked. The press had reported the killings as I had expected them to— a devil worship ritual gone horribly wrong.

The fact I was still alive and well despite Mr Clarke's promise to bring his son's killer to justice, I assume meant that Todd had acted in secret and had left no clues.

I know that assumption is a dangerous thing; and I do not rule out the possibility of a knock at my door by either the police or more likely Mr Clarke's henchmen; who would likely be more proficient than those used by poor old Todd.

I also considered carefully the blade of Nalvage and my conversation with Madimi regarding its powers.

It seemed that Madimi wanted me to use the blade. Okay in moderation, or so it seemed. However, given its power to turn the holder towards evil; I wondered if Madimi was being completely honest.

If using the blade could turn me, despite the fact I am actively destroying evil; maybe she was part of a conspiracy to trick me and push me into the arms of the Darkness. Perhaps she was a demon. A deceiver; maybe she was the daughter of the Darkness. I had to consider this a possibility.

The flip side to all of this was that I did not want to waste my life confined to my home. I had immense physical strength as a result of my power-ups; it would now take at least three strong men to physically overpower me. All of my powers were now heightened, and I did not need the blade to efficiently dispatch evildoers.

I thought back to my previous idea that I'd had while still at school. Start offering readings. I could advertise in the local paper and hire a room at a pub or community centre, and I could root out evil and punish accordingly.

Without the blade, I would not snuff out the soul, but nor would I open myself up to being corrupted. That said the blade was somehow seductive, its power immense and the thought of wielding it in anger did appeal to me.

At a foot in length, it was not easy to conceal, I could have a sheath made and strap it to my back underneath my clothing. *Yes, I had given it much thought*. It was a slightly awkward shape too.

Mr Clarke had told the press that the blade was missing; if I were caught with it, I would be immediately implicated in the murders of Todd and his henchmen and possibly even Val.

Poor Jenny was having counselling but finding that less than fruitful. Afterall she could hardly tell her councillor that the root cause of her PTSD was having seen her friend, who was a witch, slaughter three men with a knife forged by a beast slaying angel. *Padded cell already reserved.*

We maintained our friendship, and she was coping as well as could be expected between the nightmares and flashbacks.

I had used my powers to help her, but I am unable to assist with psychological disorders, nor can I cure cancer; all I can do is ease the symptoms. Strange I can trigger cancer though; we all carry it. Whether it is ever triggered is the big lottery. I can make sure that it is. I have not yet ever done that though.

The burning question— should I use my powers for good and as a side-line smite evil wherever I find it? A cross between the Equaliser and Buffy.

Should I ever again wield the blade of Nalvage?

For the next eight years, I would embrace the role of beast killer, I would wield the blade and I would almost lose my mind in the process.

The following eight years, I would call; my years of *Forlorn Absolution*.

Chapter 32
Off to a Flying Start

I placed my advert in the local Gazette.

Gifted Medium

Offers readings and spiritual Guidance

£10.00 all profits to Charity

Every Tuesdays between 8:30am & 4:00pm at the Trinity Centre, Duke Street.

Report to reception first come first served basis.

I would hire the hall and pay cash. No telephone numbers, emails and no names. I knew once people heard how good I was that business would be brisk. The Trinity Centre would for a small fee handle bookings, and the room rent was cheap as chips.

I would use my first name as it's easy to make a slip if you change that, but if asked, I would use the surname Kelly.

Obviously, I would not be slaying people at the Centre.

My first session was at 9:00a.m. the room that I was allocated was about twelve feet square with two chairs and a collapsible table. The Trinity Centre was a disused Church but still operated by the local Dioses which meant that its hallowed ground status was intact, meaning that the

Darkness could not reach or influence me while I was inside.

As I was saying, my first client arrived at 9:00a.m. she was a young woman in her early thirties. I had brought with me various paraphernalia associated with mediumship including a crystal ball, tarot cards and the like. Though in reality, I needed none of it.

I chose not to dress like some Romany Gypsy, though did dress casually with a skirt and smart V-neck mohair jumper in crimson with black and grey detailing.

As she sat opposite me, I could see that she was sad. I knew she wanted to contact someone recently departed.

Before she could speak, I said; 'Sarah is here for you.'

The woman started to cry.

'You are the real deal,' she said.

'Yes, I am.'

'I thought this would be all fake; and that you would be fishing— but you don't even know my name.'

'I don't need your name. Sarah says that she is happy where she is, but sorry that she had to leave you. She says be strong mum and yes, it is her who makes your bedside lamp flicker. It's so you know she is there with you.'

By now the woman was almost inconsolable.

'My daughter died just over six weeks ago. She had a brain tumour; she was only nine,' she managed to sob out.

'I'm so sorry—'

'Joanne—my name is Joanne, call me Jo.'

'Jo, I am so sorry for your loss—Sarah is free from the pain, she is happy, and she is with you always.'

'Is she in heaven?'

'Not quite, if she chooses to stay with you, she will remain earthbound until you die. You can release her if you choose, you can do it at any time, just tell her that you love her and that she is free to move on. No rush; just when you feel you are ready. Once you do it, you will no longer sense her presence and there will be no more flickering lights. Just remember she will not reach heaven until you tell her she is free to go; this was her choice to stay—but it is now up to you to let her go.'

'I'm not ready just yet, but I won't keep her here for much longer—thank you—'

'Cathy, my name is Cathy.'

'Can you tell her I love her?'

'You just did, and she knows it too.'

Jo handed me my ten-pound fee as she wiped her eyes and blew her nose. I felt guilty taking the money but glad I had helped her in her grief.

I was amazed that the next four clients were all decent people, no evil detected in them or in their lives. All just seeking answers from those departed loved ones.

I must have become jaded given my own experiences the world was maybe not on the brink as I had previously thought.

Next in, a face I recognised, it took me a moment as it did her. It was Alison the girl from school who'd had the squint. I suppose I should have considered I might well come across people I knew. So here we are.

'Cathy? —is it really you?' asked Ali. As she flung her arms around me.

'Yes, Ali, it is me, you look well. *She didn't.* You turned out to be a really pretty little thing, didn't you?'

'Thanks to you helping me with my eye. You look lovely too, Cathy.'

'Hey, it wasn't me it was Madimi— remember?'

'And yet here you are a medium. It was you who fixed my eye and it was you who gave Grace the lazy eye too— I know it was.'

'I'm a medium Ali, not a witch.'

'If you say so—I thank you anyway.'

'So, what are you doing here? —come on, take a seat.'

Ali was a pretty girl, very feminine, quite fine features, maybe a little on the thin side, but she looked tired, and perhaps a little stressed.

'Can you give me a reading? I need to know what my future holds.'

'Yes, I can certainly try Ali. Are you looking for me to advise you on what I see, to try and guide you? Or do you want me to say where you are likely to be in say a year or two's time?'

'I want to know where I will be in a year's time Cathy,' she replied, her voice having a tone of almost desperation, tinged with anticipation.

'Okay reach out your hand's palm up towards me.'

As I placed my hands on hers, I immediately connected.

As a rule, the majority of mediums will not break bad news. Almost without exception, they will never tell you of your own death— either the where, when or how's.

I saw all three. The where? —her home. The when? —next week. The how?—beaten to death at the hands of her boyfriend. My eyes started to fill with tears as I looked into Alison's lovely hazel eyes. I then looked down at her hands, her jacket sleeve had ridden up her arm as she'd stretched out her hands. I could see self-inflicted cuts across her arms, I let go of her hands and grabbed her left wrist, pulling her sleeve further up there were more cuts and worse still, needle marks.'

'Oh Ali—what is going on, hun?'

She pulled her arm away in shame.

'What did you see Cathy?'

'Never mind that— what I see is self-harming and drug abuse Ali. Talk to me, please.'

'You saw me dead, didn't you? I saw it in your eyes Cathy.'

'Ali what I see will only happen unless someone intervenes. It need not come true, but you need to tell me everything. How did you get to this? You were a bright girl and well-liked— except by Grace shiver mi timbers Haigh that is?'

Ali managed a smile at my Grace comment.

'I met this guy about three months ago now.'

'Right—'

'Well he was okay at first, but once we moved in together, he started to get controlling; telling me what I could wear, who I could see.'

'Mr insecurity control freak.'

Yes, then he started getting abusive, verbally at first but then he got violent too.'

'He sounds lovely Ali— why don't you leave him, what makes you stay?'

'Because he says he will kill me if I leave. He forced me to take drugs so that I would become an addict, and he'd then have even more control. He says once I'm properly hooked, he will prostitute me to his mates to pay for the drugs.'

'How long have you been taking the drugs, Ali?'

'Only a couple of weeks.'

'Well I can cure you of your addiction particularly as it is still early days; but it won't cure you of this piece of shit.'

'I don't know what to do Cathy.'

'What does he do for a living Ali?'

'I think this is what he does. He prays on girls like me and then gets them hooked on drugs and then prostitutes them.'

'What makes you think that?'

'I've heard him on the phone, he seems less cagy now, since he started me on drugs.'

'Wow, you certainly know how to pick them Ali—'

'Tell me about it—what do you think I should do? I just don't know which way to turn.'

'Well we had our little secret before, so let me sort this for you too. Can you go and stay with your mum for a day or two?'

'He won't like it.'

'Well, tell him your mum is ill and you must go. Make sure you have an alibi Ali. Give me your address and go to your mums, do not go back to your place. Write your address on here look and leave it with me. We never had this conversation Ali.'

'What will you do?' asked Ali as she scribbled her address in my notebook.'

'I'm not sure— it will depend on him I guess.'

'Will you hurt him?'

'Never you mind Ali— will he be at home now?'

'Yes, I told him I was popping to the shops.'
'What's his name?'
'Oliver— his name is Oliver.'
'Okay, you get to your mums and make sure lots of people see you together— go.'
'Okay— be careful he is a nasty piece of work.'
'I'm sure he is— Ali, you can never come here again or try and contact me— do you promise.'

Ali threw her arms around me again.

Thanks, Cathy—I love you.'
'Yeah, I love you too, Ali.'

I decided to pop home, collect my blade and change into something more appropriate for my little ruse.

An hour later, I was knocking at the door of the address given to me by Ali.

'You forgot your key again you stupid fucking bitch.' Shouted Oliver as he unlocked the door.

'Hi— You must be Oliver— I'm a friend of Ali's— is she in?' I asked.

Oliver looked a little dumbstruck his eyes widening as he looked at my exposed cleavage and mini skirt.

'She's down the shops,' he replied as he processed what his eyes were seeing.

'Can I come in and wait?' I asked with a cheeky little smile.

'Sure, come on in. Have a seat,' he said directing me to his lounge.

I had not been sure what to expect. The apartment was a good size and well furnished, I suppose if you are trying to come over as a respectable, nice guy, there is little point bringing a girl to a dirty squat. Oliver was clean, smartly dressed and looked like he could handle himself.

I took a seat on the couch; he parked himself directly across from me in a chair. *Obvious why*. I obliged by opening my legs slightly to give him a glimpse of the goods.

'Ali never said you were coming over. What's your name?'

'Cathy—no I didn't tell her— I thought I'd make it a surprise.'

'Well, she has some beautiful looking friends if you're anything to go by.'

'Ali is a pretty girl though, don't you think?'

'Yes, but you're something else.'

'Thanks— I bet you're a bit of a stud, I can tell you know.'

'I don't know about that. I do alright.'

'Really— because I'd fuck you right now if Ali wasn't due back.'

Oliver's face was a picture, he picked his phone up to text Ali; as he did, he saw her message saying she'd gone to her mums.

'Oh, as luck would have it, she's gone to her mums for a couple of days as her mum seems to be unwell.'

'So, we can party then?'

'We most certainly can—'

'Great— do you have any Charlie or anything? if we're going to party, we may as well do it right.'

Oliver was nearly cumming in his pants. At that moment, he would have done anything. He went to his wall safe in his bedroom and opened it. There was cash, heroin and cocaine as well as a 9 mm automatic.

At this point, I was undecided how this was going to play out other than Oliver would definitely have to die.

He was evil, so using the blade would be safe. If I killed him some other way using my powers, it would need to be in self-defence; or it's straight to hell for me.

So, option one was gut him with the blade and make it look like a robbery or drug-related gang killing. Receive a power-up and end an evil soul.

Option two would be to provoke a potentially murderous response and then kill him using my powers, no power-up or evil soul ended.

Option three—

Oliver pulled out some cocaine from the safe, leaving the safe door open. He cut four lines of coke and gave me a rolled up fifty. I took two lines. He did the same, and then we got down to business. We fucked hard for two hours. He was pretty fucking good, and I had been ready for it.

'Fuck you are good,' said Oliver.

'I know I am— and I will say Ollie— you are in my top five best ever fucks.

'Is that good is it?'

'I would say so yes I'm easily into three figures so you can give yourself a well-deserved pat on the back.'

'What now?'

'Well now we've done the business we can talk business.'

'What business?'

Well, let's discuss Ali, shall we?' I said indignantly.

'What do you mean? — what about Ali?'

'Well I've just fucked her man; I feel a little guilty if I'm honest. Don't you?'

'No—In fact you know what— if you will be my woman, I will just blow her out, she doesn't mean that much to me. It's just a casual relationship we both fuck other people. You though— fuck you're something else— be my woman and you will want for nothing; I'd treat you like my queen.'

'I get that a lot, I have a similar offer from a Prince— No really I do! — The thing is Ali told me that you are abusive and have got her hooked on heroin so that you can pimp her out— is that true?'

Oliver looked a little confused.

'She said that did she? — lying little slut.'

'Well, you do have a safe full of smack, cash and a gun.'

'So, what—I sell drugs to people with money; I'm a high-end dealer. The gun is for protection. Why are you getting all holier than thou? You just did two lines of coke and fucked your so-called friends' boyfriend for two hours solid.'

'I just needed a fuck to be honest Ollie— I think maybe I should call the police.'

Oliver jumped out of bed and pulled his gun from the safe.

'You ain't calling nobody bitch.'

'Or else what?'

'Or else I will kill you.'

I reached my phone from my bag and began to dial. Oliver cocked the gun.

'Put the phone down you messed up cunt, or I swear I will shoot you in the fucking face.'

'No, you won't because you can't pull the trigger.'

Oliver squeezed the trigger— well he tried at least. I had control of him now. I was still undecided as to his fate.

Witch assisted suicide like I'd done with Michael. Perhaps I should prepare a heroin fix for him and make him overdose; or maybe just slay him with the blade.

'What the fuck are you doing—how can you even do this?' asked Oliver as he stared helplessly at his frozen outstretched arm.

Yes, this was the Enochian magic the Darkness had shown me. Yes, I needed bodily fluids, and yes, I had them, just not from biting his lip.

'Because Oliver I am a fucking witch and you despite being a pretty amazing fuck are an evil piece of shit, and you are going to die here today. I just need to decide how.'

'Take the money— I'll leave Ali alone I promise, you don't have to do this.'

'Yes, Oliver, I do. In fact, it's not that I have to— it's that I want to.'

'What sort of sick bitch are you?'

'The sickest kind Oliver.'

'Can't we just talk it over? There must be another way.'

'Oliver you prey on vulnerable women, you gain their trust, and then you get them hooked on heroin before pimping them out— and you call me sick.'

'I provide a service, girls like Ali are in high demand. If I didn't do it someone else would.'

'That makes it alright, does it? —that is your justification for using and hurting my friend.'

'If You kill me someone else will take up the slack— you won't change anything really.'

'It will mean Ali is safe, and that's enough for me.'

I was still naked as I walked around the bedroom chiding Oliver; there was a good reason for that.

'Look at it this way, Oliver— you are going to die, but you just had the best fucking sex of your entire, sick, sadistic life. What a way to go out.'

'Fuck you!'

'That's what they all Say Ollie, and you just did at least get to fuck me— which is more than most of the others ever managed.'

I pulled the blade from my bag and turned to face Oliver.

'What the fuck is that?'

'It's a knife Ollie— an exceptional knife in fact.'

'A knife's a knife. Have you ever killed anyone, or am I your first?'

'I'll tell you what— cards on the table— I'll tell you my secrets if you tell me yours, let's have a bad deed amnesty.'

'Like what?'

'How many girls like Ali have you sold into a life of prostitution?'

'Ten— maybe more,' replied Ollie dismissively.

'How many girls have died from overdoses or beatings?'

Oliver said nothing.

'You have killed Oliver. I can see it; it's written all over your face— how many?'

Oliver again said nothing.

'Okay I don't think you get the principal of this amnesty— so let me have my turn— I have killed four people with this blade alone— back to you— how many girls have you killed Oliver?'

Oliver now looked a little more concerned— a little more frightened at what I had just divulged.

'Tell me or I swear I'll castrate you where you stand.'

'One girl— that's all— I swear!'

'That's one too many Ollie—how did she die? —'

Ollie stared at the blade and said nothing.

'You beat her to death, didn't you? You have a temper, and you would have killed Ali too. I saw it— that is why I'm here.'

'I never meant to kill her— I just couldn't stop myself— I just lose it sometimes when I'm angry.'

'Well, it won't happen again Ollie of that you can be sure.'

'What's so special about your knife? — you obviously don't fucking need it,' said Ollie as he looked at the gun in his hand.

'This my dear Ollie is the blade of Nalvage it will kill you and destroy your soul in the process.'

'What?'

'Well if I killed you with your gun for example— your soul would live on, it may go to hell, it may achieve redemption, or it may even be reincarnated. Killing you with the blade means you cease to have ever been.'

I was now stood toe to toe with Oliver. I took the gun from his hand and threw it on the bed.

'Who the fuck are you?'

'I am Catherine Antoinette Heely; self-proclaimed slayer of evil— endorsed by the angel Madimi.'

'You're fucking mental is what you are— fucking angels— you need locking up you crazy fucking bitch, you're just a fucking Psycho— go on then do it,' spat Ollie in fear and frustration, as he stood fixed to the spot, frozen in place by my Enochian magic.

The blade in my hand was resonating with excitement and anticipation; it was inches away from evil, and it wanted blood, it wanted a soul.

Was this me? Is this what I had become? A cold, calculating killer— I knew that if I killed Oliver I would be embarking on a whole new chapter in my life. I would be heading down a very dark road indeed— a road which may lead me directly into the arms of the Darkness. *It just felt so right!*

I had always believed that all life is precious, my experiences over the years had taught me otherwise. Ali's life was precious; she was a good person. Oliver would have killed her given a chance. I absolutely would not allow that to happen.

Did I though, have the right to end his life so completely and irreversibly? Was I becoming a monster? The blade did make me feel murderous, just being near to it made me giddy and hedonistic. I was confused by how I felt— I should not feel excited, I should not feel aroused at the prospect of taking a life, regardless of the fact it was evil.

My momentary deliberations must have given Oliver a glimpse of false hope. But it was deliberation and not as he'd hoped, hesitation.

'You can't do it, can you? — you're having second thoughts,' said Ollie with a slight sound of relief in his voice.

As I looked Oliver in the eyes, I smiled. I inhaled long and slow, momentarily closing my eyes as I did.

'WRONG!' I replied as I opened my eyes wide.

Before he could utter another word, the blade at my side; in one swift and continuous action rose up and then sliced down at a forty-five-degree angle across the side of

Ollie's neck. A gaping wound five or so inches long and two inches deep opened up.

The arterial spray from the final beats of his pounding, fear-filled heart covered me. I could taste the adrenalin as my open mouth accepted his lifeblood. I see now why the Alpha wolf takes the heart of the prey; gorged as it is, in adrenaline after the chase.

As I collected my power-up from the blade; my body shook with almost orgasmic pleasure. Oliver's now soulless body fell to the floor.

I stood over his body naked. I was covered from head to toe in his warm, sticky blood.

As the sensations subsided, I calmly showered and dressed. Cleaning the scene of my presence as best I could. I know that I am not on the DNA database, nor have I ever been fingerprinted; I would need to be a suspect in the first place in order to be put at the scene.

I had brought a wig with me; if I was seen leaving Ollie's apartment, the description would be that of a redhead.

I left the contents of the safe in situ; the scene would hopefully be baffling to the police, not robbery unless the robbers had panicked as Oliver reached for his gun. It was evident by the blood spatter that someone had stood with Oliver as he'd bled out. This would make it look as though it was personal; along with the fact there would be no signs of forced entry.

Ali had a sound alibi, although I doubt that she would even be a suspect. She was after all a trainee prostitute for Oliver's sex trafficking business; so unlikely he would have documented the fact.

As a criminal no doubt known to the police, I figured—well hoped actually; that the police probably wouldn't be looking to throw much in the way of resources at solving the case; that's how I saw it at any rate.

I would become more and more proficient over the coming years; at both killing and covering my tracks.

It seemed that my first *clinic had been* a success; I had helped five people find closure over the loss of loved ones, and I had saved the life of an old friend, at the same time taking an evil piece of shit out of the picture. A good day's work by any standard.

Chapter 33
2018:   The Canning Case

It had been some twelve years since Steph, and I had first met.

After the traumatic events back in 2006 with DCI Lyons and DCI Salter. Followed in 2008 by Todd's attempted revenge. I had backed off from getting involved with Steph's stories.

It had now been two years since I ended my years of *Forlorn Absolution*, and I was now living a solitary life. Though my eight years as a finder and punisher of evildoers had been mostly rewarding in the end as always seemed to be the case, those I loved had ended up suffering. I could bear it no more.

Steph and I maintained our friendship; though she was mostly in the dark regarding my activities throughout my Forlorn Absolution period.

Steph would still call to see me; though her visits were far less frequent. She would Stopover occasionally.

Steph was now a very successful journalist. Her exposé articles had won her awards around the world.

Steph's stories were always tremendous. Never about a local councillor fiddling a hundred pounds in expenses. They were always multi-million-pound criminal enterprises; usually but not always drug-related.

Steph travelled a great deal and was often working undercover. As such, we saw each other less and less. She had recently spent eighteen months in South America. Her reasons for leaving to run away from her guilt at the death of her friend and informant Zoe Canning.

Steph had called to see me in the spring of 2018 and was seeking my spiritual insight to the case, she wanted to bring to justice those responsible for Zoe's death though I was unable to cast much light on the situation, but assured her I would keep the channels open.

It was then late 2018 when I next heard from Steph; receiving as I did a telephone call from her.

'Cathy. I know it's been a while. I need a favour.'

'What sort of favour Steph?'

'Well, you remember Zoe, who died a couple of years ago?'

'You mean Zoe, who was murdered two years ago.'

'Yes, that one.'

'What about it?'

'I am in a relationship with her husband. I know what you're going to say. But it's the real deal.'

'Go on—'

'Well, his daughter is receiving messages from Zoe. They do seem to be the real deal. But it has been two years, and I wonder why it's suddenly started.'

'Well there has likely been a trigger— maybe even the fact you are sleeping with her husband.'

'You think?'

'It is possible— maybe she has a message it may not be negative.'

'Well, would you do a reading for Steve— Pretty please. Just for me. It would mean so much, and it might give him the closure that he is looking for.'

'Well, as it's you. And you asked so nicely. Don't be a stranger Steph I miss you.'

'When shall I say.'

'Tell him to pop over this afternoon if he wants. I'm always here, you know that.'

Less than an hour later there was a ring of my doorbell. *He must be keen.*

'You must be Steve.' I smiled as I reached out to shake his hand, 'I'm Cathy, please come in.'

I had lit a cinnamon candle and placed it centrally on my coffee table.

'Shall I take my shoes off?' asked Steve.

'If you don't mind. Please take a seat. Can I get you a drink before we start?'

'No, I'm fine thanks.'

'Okay. Steph has explained things to me. So, before we start, I need to just prepare myself, just a few cleanse and protection prayers and rituals.'

'Whatever you need to do. It's all new to me.'

As I was preparing, I could sense his thoughts. He was having a good look around the place. He had clocked that I had no wedding or engagement ring. He looked at the floor in the hallway. Looking for food bowls. *Typical.*

'No black cat! And I don't have a broomstick, cauldron or pointy hat either!' I said with a knowing smile.

Steve looked shocked. 'What, you read minds?'

'Not quite. It was written all over your face! It's your first time, I take it?'

'Err, yes, it is. Sorry I didn't mean—'

'Mean what? You didn't say anything, did you?'

I completed my white light protection prayers.

'Take your jacket off and lay it over the arm of the chair please.'

I offered Steve my hands, palms up, inviting him to place his hands on mine.

Steve complied with my unspoken instruction.

As I looked into Steve's eyes, I could see something very familiar to me. I could see the mark of the Darkness. Effectively a label saying property of the Darkness. Do not touch. Steve was marked. He had sold his soul.

Steve seemed like a really nice guy. But for whatever reason, he had sold out to the Darkness. This could mean my friend Steph was in danger. Or it could be completely unrelated. He may never be asked to repay his debt to the Darkness. If he was asked to repay the debt. The cost was usually high and more than most can bear.

I pulled my hands away. I knew what it was. But I couldn't tell him. The Darkness would have felt my connection.

'Steve, I am sorry, but I cannot give you a reading.'

Steve looked confused and rightly so. 'Why not? We've only just started!' asked Steve, surprised by the sudden change. 'What's wrong?'

'I'm not sure exactly. But there seems to be a Darkness around you. Maybe you are in a bad place emotionally. Maybe you have made or are about to make a decision that will have serious consequences. Whatever it is, I cannot see past it.'

'I have no idea what you are talking about. I have been in a dark place since I lost my wife, but recently things have improved significantly, so that makes no sense to me.'

'Steve, I really am sorry, but there is nothing more I can do or say. It's probably best that you leave.'

'Whoa, back up a minute! What is going on? I thought you were genuine. Steph said you were good at this.' Steve was clearly upset and confused by my response.

'This was all just bullshit! Is there any wonder I don't believe in this bollocks!'

'Tell me what it is Cathy. I just don't get it.' Said Steve as he put on his shoes and jacket.

'Steve, take some solace knowing that Zoe is communicating with you through Faith. She will be unable to contact you directly for the same reason I can't give you a reading or contact Zoe in your presence.'

'So why is this happening all of a sudden? Zoe has been gone for two years. Why is she communicating now?'

'There has clearly been a trigger event, Steve. She is now trying to guide you with messages as that is her only route, using Faith as the conduit.'

'What trigger event?'

'I don't know Steve, and that's the truth, but Zoe is trying to help and protect you.'

'Okay, I've heard enough. Thanks for your time.' said Steve as he opened the door to leave.

'Be wary, Steve. I fear you have let someone into your life who is not looking out for your best interests.'

Steve simply shook his head as he walked away down the path. I closed the door and locked it behind him.

I sat and pondered. I could not tell Steve what I saw. But Steph. She knew what I knew. I could tell her. Indeed, I must tell her. She may be in danger.

After some deliberation, I decided to call Steph. The call went directly to her voicemail.

'Hi Steph, it's Cathy. I need to speak to you ASAP. Please call me when you get this. I am just going to grab a quick shower, so give me half an hour.

Having showered, I sat in my chair, checking my phone for any missed calls or texts. There were none. I settled down for the evening with a green tea. Replaying the earlier events in my mind. Suddenly, there was a long continuous buzz from my doorbell.

'Coming!' *I bet this is Steph.*

When I woke, I found myself bound. My hands tied above my head with my washing line. The bindings had me stretched and my feet per partially lifted from the floor.

The dressing gown I was wearing was open as the belt had been knotted in the middle and used as a gag.

As I focused. I could see two men. More accurately, I could see a man and with him the Darkness. I knew it was him. He appeared human. But that was for everyone else's benefit. I saw his true form. This dark energy that had tormented me for my entire life. He was here for me. He had grown impatient of waiting and clearly knew I had seen his interest in Steve Canning.

His associate, a sleazy looking individual, was clearly here to do the torture as the Darkness is unable to directly harm humans, physically at least. Unless he possesses a physical body.

This was the final showdown. He was here to turn me or kill me in the process. This would require all of my powers. I would not go down without a fight.

'Listen Cathy I am going to remove your gag so that we can talk. If you scream, our next stop will be your sister's. She can watch her two children die horribly before we gut her. Do you understand?'

I nodded vigorously as his sidekick removed my gag.

'Hello, Catherine. You know who I am, don't you?' asked the Darkness as he approached me.

I again nodded. 'I know what you are! —'

-See how this concludes in Sold Out /Soul Doubt, book 1 of the 'When Darkness calls' series. -

Acknowledgements

Other than my own existing knowledge and fertile imagination, the following were referenced.

The King James Version of the bible ISBN 978-1-61624-518-2 from Barbour PublishingInc.

John Dee & the Empire of Angels by Jason Louv ISBN978-1-62055-589-7

Daemonologie a critical edition; King James by Brett R Warren ISBN-13: 978-1532968914

A little more about me, the author.

Never for a moment did I ever consider that I might become an author.

Many might well read this book and say that I am not one.

I wasted my school years and only really fared well in practical subjects though my English teacher said I had a good turn of phrase and was constantly disappointed in my lack of effort.

I have spent years writing technical documents but had a story in my head for some 20 years which I finally managed to put to print in 2019 (Sold Out/Soul Doubt) I then discovered I had the bug and wanted to write more.

I try and write as I like to read; that is pacy stories that are easy to follow and relate to and which deliver a strong message about morality.

I genuinely want to reach as many people as possible and to encourage those who don't generally read to pick up my books and relate to the characters' struggles.

I won't use 50 words when 10 will suffice I am trying to tell a story not impress the reader with my intellect and vocabulary.

I truly hope you enjoy the book and would welcome your comments by email to jemartinfictionauthor@gmail.com

Printed in Great Britain
by Amazon